JINX

A Catherine Kint Mystery

HUGH MCGINLAY

Clan Destine
PRESS

This edition published by Clan Destine Press in 2021
First published by Threekookaburras 2015

Clan Destine Press
PO Box 121, Bittern
Victoria, 3918 Australia

National Library of Australia Cataloguing-In-Publication data:

McGinlay, Hugh

Jinx

ISBN: 978-0-6450021-6-4 (paperback)
ISBN: 978-0-6450021-9-5 (eBook)

Cover Design by © Willsin Rowe
Design & Typesetting by Clan Destine Press

Clan Destine
P R E S S

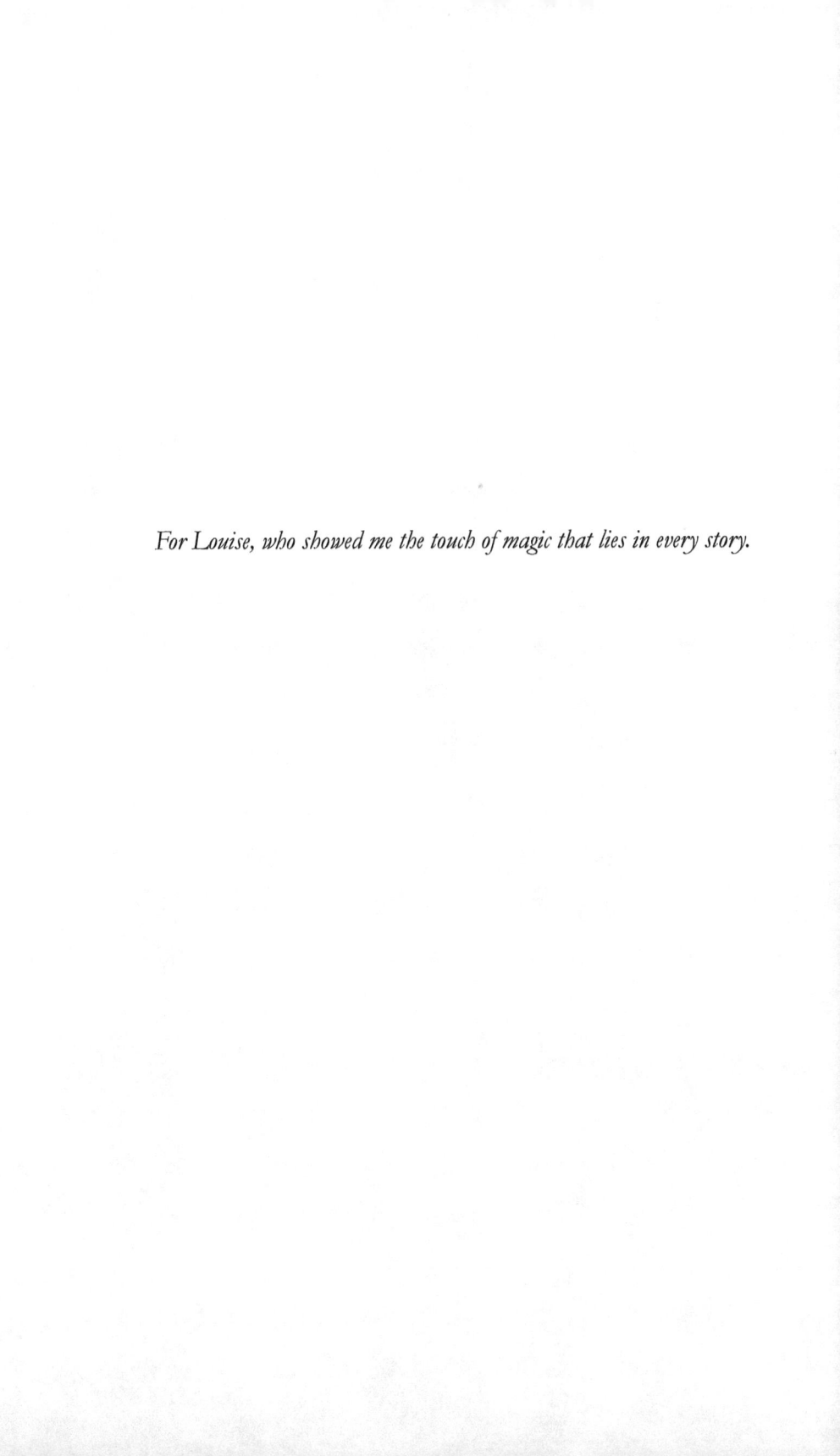

For Louise, who showed me the touch of magic that lies in every story.

1

People who don't mix business and pleasure took bad career advice.
~ Catherine Kint

Had she been religious she would have said a prayer. It was dastardly, it was cruel and it was unjust. It was spread everywhere, covering everything, going against nature and defying all that was correct.

Surely, Catherine thought, *there was no need for this much hollandaise.* And yet it was there, perfect, in front of her.

Catherine Kint was at that moment sitting on the bench of an eatery in the north of Melbourne, taking in the ambience, eggs benedict, the newspaper and large amounts of life-giving coffee. While the ambience was doing little, therapeutically speaking, all other elements were exorcising her hangover and lifting her mood. She had made a deal with herself about the hangover (it being her fifth in as many days) in which she would reconcile with it, and its side order of regret, after breakfast. Then she would plan an attack for the mounting work that was plaguing three corners of her mind. For now though, it was just her, the hollandaise and the coffee. Alone, and almost at peace.

As minutes became tens of minutes, and they became clusters of tens of minutes, the mosquito-in-the-tent irritability that had dogged her since waking was receding as surely as the barista's hairline.

Instinct caused her to turn momentarily and look towards the room, seeing newspapers rapidly fluttered in front of two men on separate tables. A moment to check their body language told Catherine there was nothing but admiration in their glances; she caught sight of her own reflection in the dark metal of the coffee machine and smiled. The hangover didn't show, just a slim woman with a Mod bob haircut and dark eyes. Perhaps her slow burn contentment was alluring, and they appreciated the languid way she turned her newspaper page, or the way her dark fringe danced in time as she nodded agreement to one of the more astute opinion pieces. Maybe they enjoyed watching a woman contemplating her position on the planet at that time, and finding it increasingly satisfactory.

Her contemplation was ended by the locust of the twenty-first century: her mobile rang.

The news on the line was bad.

If Boris had been screaming, or crying, Catherine would have been less worried. Instead, he spoke with a detachment Catherine had only ever heard him use moments before vomiting. Boris – raconteur, friend and barman – was obviously upset.

'I hope you've started without me.'

'I have, of course.'

'Catherine, I'm looking at a dead girl.'

'Where are you?'

'Alleyway near the Abruzzo.'

'On my way.'

'Catherine…'

'Yes?'

'She's…'

'She's what, Boris?'

'She's… Christ… she's had her throat cut, Catherine.'

'You called the cops?'

'Yeah. Jesus.'

By the time Boris had uttered his final blasphemies, Catherine had peeled a twenty from her wallet, finished her latte and was out the door. She had ascertained from this conversation that:

a) Something horrible had happened.

b) Boris was in no state to be alone, as he was possibly about to vomit on a corpse. Nor was he able to say exactly where he was. Was it the alley behind the Abruzzo Club or the T-junction of alleyways near the Abruzzo car park?

c) She would be a better friend if she moved immediately to wherever he was; the cafe was only a hop, skip or a jump from either place.

d) Work was going to have to wait.

Catherine walked briskly in the Melbourne spring morning, watching the birds on the power lines and listening to the rumbling traffic, her mind moving through the possibilities of what the next minutes would show. She tried the car park alley first. Considering the two possibilities, she thought the T-junction was more likely to be a crime scene. It was better concealed, for one thing, and reeked of possibility. The possibility of lust, of garbage, of the odd student desk, even the possibility of blood.

Catherine arrived just as the yawp of sirens came from the south. She saw two figures sitting, one facing the other and one slumped, surrounded by dried blood. Blood sprayed over the ground in curved lines around the body as it fell. A woman who had been young and beautiful. The blood that hadn't circled her body stained her torso and pooled around the nearest cobblestones. Her right arm lay across her body; her right hand was missing the middle, ring and little fingers. Her mouth was slack. Her dark eyes were still open.

Opposite her, Boris was breathing deeply, his bulk folded into an uncharacteristically compact unit as he stared. The parts of his face not covered by his light brown beard were pale. His eyes blinked often, but his line of vision remained consistent. About a metre of cobblestones separated his boots from the outermost circle of blood. Catherine suspected she could cross his path of vision or even pinch him but he would not stop looking at the figure opposite him.

'Boris.'

'I'm all right. Thanks for coming.'

He would be all right – he hadn't even vomited. Catherine raised her gaze above his head, where a nail protruded from the wooden fence bordering the alley. Fixed to the nail was what looked like a small sheaf of wheat stained with spots of blood. Then she looked at the woman.

Catherine's eyes went soft as she took it all in. She felt the synapses of a previous career twang and crackle. Part of her fought it, reminded her that she wasn't that job anymore. She kept looking. The cool air seemed to hold more light than usual. Catherine wondered if she could smell the blood. No, just fresh air, pollen and cold cobblestones.

She moved closer. Not close enough to touch – that was for police, which had never been her job – but to absorb all she could. Only if needed, only for the interview.

She'd bled out, as victims of throat injuries often did. The coagulation told Catherine that the wound was at least an hour old, but it could be many more. It would be impossible to say without an autopsy. Her carotid artery had been neatly sliced along with the rest of her throat, the wound continuing across the neck to her right ear. Judging by the amount of blood that stained the cobblestones, where her singular finger now pointed, she'd lost blood from the wound in her throat before her fingers had been severed. Catherine was painfully aware how long it had been since this had been her job. Her experience with crime scene investigation meant she could read things here, but that suddenly felt a long time ago. Catherine shook her head slightly, pushing away the idea of all the things she was missing.

Her head was tilted back, showing the opened neck. Her dark eyes seemed focused and low, as if she were staring at something above Boris.

The wounds on the right hand were clean. A single blade, a knife – likely the same knife that slit her throat. Catherine couldn't see the fingers nearby. Scanning the bloodstains, she noted three spots where blood had spurted in three arcs of diminishing distance. They were consistent with the body's current position. They had been cut while she sat here, after the death.

Her black hair was long and straight, partially tied back in a loose ponytail. She was wearing lipstick and, Catherine decided, just a hint too much eyeliner, though her foundation was perfect for her tanned complexion. Double checking her theory on time of death, and murmuring an apology to the police, Catherine gently touched the dead girl's forehead – it was cold. This had happened hours ago.

The woman seemed familiar to Catherine; maybe she had been on television. She was in her twenties, dressed in jeans, leather belt, pale brown jacket over a black cotton top, a scarf of many colours that may have been purchased in Vietnam, Collingwood, or both. Somewhere a raven called an expletive.

Catherine followed the murdered woman's eyes. She had been staring at the wheat hanging from the fence opposite her. Three visible spots of flecked blood stained the golden stem and ears.

Two police came hurrying up the alleyway. Boris began to move as they came close, standing slowly like an old man rising for the national anthem. His movement did not disturb the wheat behind him. The terse-looking constable with the blonde bob approached quickest.

'Move back, miss.' Her voice sounded brisk.

Catherine turned, and took two steps back. 'Good morning, officer.'

She was appalled that her voice wavered. She knew it was understandable in the circumstances, but she found it disappointing.

'Move over here, please. You too, sir.' Boris moved next to Catherine, three metres away from the body.

'Did you find her?'

There was no waver in the cop's voice. Her partner meanwhile moved up the alley, speaking into his radio. He was tall and kept shifting his head as he peered down the long alley.

Catherine motioned to Boris. 'No, he did.'

Boris gave a little wave.

The cop realised that Boris was in shock, and turned to Catherine. 'When did he find her?'

'I got a call fifteen minutes ago.'

'Why did he call you?'

'He was running late for breakfast.'

'Your name, please?'

'Kint. I'm Catherine Kint.'

The cop's pen paused halfway to her pad. 'I know that name. You're police?'

'No, I'm a milliner; I was CSI for a few years. Unsworn.'

The cop's eyebrows knitted and she smiled. 'And now you make hats?'

Catherine raised a palm. 'Permanent sea change.'

This was clearly enough. 'Did you touch anything?'

'No, I didn't – I was just making sure Boris was OK. Before you guys came.'

'Do either of you know the victim?'

Catherine looked to Boris, who seemed mesmerised with watching the tall cop tape off the scene.

'Not me. Boris?'

He turned back to the body while he answered the question. 'No, I don't know her.'

'What's your name?'

'Boris Shakhovskoy.'

'Russian?'

'My Dad is. I'm from here.'

'When did you find her?'

'Just before I rang triple O,' he checked his watch. 'Twenty minutes?'

'Why were you coming this way?'

Catherine turned back to the body as Boris answered more questions. She longed for a gin; worrying about hangovers suddenly felt indulgent. The woman's handbag was still by her side. In that handbag would be identification, a name. A name that would lead to family, friends, parents.

She moved to Boris, who had finished giving his details, and put an arm around him. He leaned into her and exhaled softly. Comforting, thought Catherine, was the only thing she needed to be. Even so, there was something in the way the cop was staring at the girl, and then trying to take notes with a pen that wouldn't work, that churned her gut. Made her want to be a part of the machine that made scenes like this make sense. As much as any person or machine could.

Catherine turned back to the victim. Her dead eyes staring at the spattered wheat. It looked like a challenge, or a warning. As if the girl was an arrow towards this symbol. A bloody arrow.

Later, once she had pledged to breathe police station air, drink police station coffee and to give an official statement, Catherine walked home. Boris hadn't felt like breakfast.

Just three years earlier that had been a daily event. Working the scene of a death. Crime scene investigation was a life of fact-checking and staring into the eyes of dead strangers. Cataloguing facts of a person's demise, to be cross-checked by the police and the coroner. Catherine remembered the busyness of such scenes. She wondered if back then she would have felt as shaken as she did today, or was it just the time elapsed since she had last been at the scene of a murder? Perhaps death was easier when you had a job to do.

Entering her apartment, she scratched her cat's neck, put the kettle on and ran the shower. Her mind churned over the morning's events. Catherine knew the victim would have lived long enough to see her blood spray from her body. What the victim had seen, felt and thought as the knife came across her throat haunted her.

These images were front and centre, but were continually interrupted by the ocean-like chatter rising from a brain that was trying to drown a terrible event. The chatter only noticed in the quiet that holds the mind for hours after a consciousness-changing event. Catherine wondered if Boris would be at the pub tonight to verify her story. How long had he stared at the body before he'd rung her? How much knowledge of blood had she lost in three years? Is it ridiculous to say that juice is to tomatoes as blood to humans? If tomatoes had only been introduced to Europe in the eighteenth century did it really mean that Shakespeare never had a BLT, and if so, how could his world view be so broad?

She kept coming back to the body and the fingers. They would be centre stage of her brain for a while. Time was the thing. Once time had passed, the body would be a memory only arising every now and again. The police would find who committed this murder and she would understand the horror. That would have to be enough on this one. There was no connection to her aside from the fact that her best friend had found the body.

She breathed in as she pushed a towel through her hair. She looked at the framed photos that punctuated the pale walls of her bedroom. Memories become photos become furniture become background, until someone dies and they awaken. As she walked back into the living area the light seemed to flood her. It all seemed temporary; the fact that it existed at all was suddenly miraculous.

Catherine made a pot of Earl Grey tea and settled in her favourite chair, excellent for lounging and the perfect distance between her phone, bookshelf, fish bowl, television, stereo and liquor cabinet. She had missed a call while in the shower – a blocked number. Waiting for the voicemail, she anticipated a work-related message. Something about the new brim block she was expecting, or a late order for the spring racing carnival. More normal, a girl deserves a bit of normal.

All things considered, Melissa sounded calm. 'Catherine it's me. I've just handed my passport to police. They've questioned me over the murder of a girl called Cassandra. She was killed in the alley behind my house last night. They're going to search my house. I'm freaking out here. Can we meet?'

2

There is little that can be done, that hasn't been done, except to you.
~ Boris Shakhovskoy

Lunch hour was in full swing when they entered the crowded Lebanese bakery on Sydney Road. Melissa dominated the room even while trying to keep a low profile. There was something about six-inch heels on a heavily tattooed woman with a shock of black hair that got people to look up from their tables. Although tiny in size, she usually walked as if she owned the world, but today her stride was less confident. Eventually they sat in a corner with their spinach triangles. Catherine noticed Melissa was wearing less makeup than usual, and her watery green eyes had little of their usual zest.

They'd met years ago, on a mushroom-gathering trip arranged by Melissa's former housemate who had fancied Catherine. Neither Catherine nor Melissa saw him anymore – a bad lover and a worse housemate – but their friendship had been firmly forged. The mushrooms had been delicious. The pair had survived some ups and downs. Upon Melissa's giving up booze she had taken up a worse vice: celebrity. It seemed to Catherine that Melissa's every waking moment was geared towards raising her own profile as a "rock-star witch" in the local media. Catherine had no issue with anyone pursuing his or her desires, but if that desire was fame, it made for painfully shallow conversation. Despite this, their friendship had remained solid, with Catherine always warming to Melissa's ability to tell a story well, as she was doing now.

'I guess I should have seen this coming. Actually I did, but it was murky – one of those storms that you can't do anything about anyway,' Melissa said.

'So you knew this might happen?'

'A couple of weeks ago I came back from a trip to the bush and found the back window ajar. My mind was scattered because I had been fasting for three days and had encountered some strange things, as I do.' Mel hesitated, as she did sometimes when she realised she was talking like an idiot. 'My cat Magus was wandering around outside looking very pleased with himself because he'd got out. Purring triumphantly. So I went in, and sure enough, someone had been through the place.'

'Why didn't you tell me?'

'Didn't think much of it – nothing had been taken, or so I thought. I guessed it might have been local kids having a joke with the witch down the street. Then I found the doll.'

'The doll?' Catherine leaned forward.

'Just your run of the mill baby's doll, but she had the fingers on one hand cut off.'

'The same three fingers as the body this morning?' Catherine hadn't noticed, but she was gripping the table.

'So that ugly cop told me.'

'So you…'

'I was worried then – it's a powerful symbol – but I studied it and there was no magic on it. No traces of power, nothing. I thought of blogging about it but I was already getting heaps of hits from my post on familiars; didn't want to cross-pollinate. I was actually going to bring it up this week, on my Channel 31 show.'

'It wouldn't be a warning of some kind?'

'I figured it was just someone messing with me, but I like it when they try and get in my face; means I'm winning. I just had it out on the porch, just to show I wasn't afraid. Where it was, next to my front door earlier when the police came.'

'That was quick, were they door-knocking the whole street?'

'Must have been. I opened the door and the cop was already looking at the doll. Asked me about the significance of the cut fingers. I told him what I told you and suddenly it was a full interview, search warrant, and can we keep your passport.'

'Hell.'

'Indeed.' Melissa took a sip of her coffee, and looked at the glass, turning it in her hand. Her spinach triangle was left untouched.

'It could be the best publicity of my life, but I don't like the coincidence. I didn't kill her. Catherine, I like the spotlight, and I hated Cassandra, but I didn't kill her.'

'Wait, so you knew her?'

Melissa looked up from the table. 'You remember that trouble I had with the real-estate agent?'

'That was her?'

'Apparently.'

'And she died near your house?'

'I had nothing to do with it.'

'No, it doesn't make sense that you would actually kill someone you called a vile maggot in a tribunal room.'

Melissa's eyes were downcast. 'I'm not sure that Hansard extends to VCAT, but yes, it was recorded.'

'And then there was the article in the *Express*.'

'I was misquoted.'

'So you didn't put a spell on her, then announce it?'

Mel's eyes remained fixed at the table's surface. 'I told all the papers, but only the *Express* went with it.'

'It was still very unwise, even before this. So did you ring the police?'

Melissa shook her head. 'I didn't even know she was dead until they knocked on my door.'

'I mean after your house was broken into?'

'Y'know, I was going to call when this voice inside me says, "Don't call the cops – there's going to be a really hard time with some cops soon", so I didn't. That's what I meant when I said I saw it coming, kind of.'

There was a long pause as Catherine took in what Mel had said. If you could bottle moments like these.

'OK, that aside, you've been arrested because of a doll? There must be more to it.'

Melissa passed a rolled cigarette from hand to hand and looked outside to where she would be able to smoke. 'Then there's my knife.'

Catherine could feel a vein throbbing in her temple. 'Go on.'

'Do you remember the ornamental knives I had in my parlour?'

'Two knives with pearl handles mounted on a green and red shield with a Polish inscription on them. Yes, I remember them.'

Melissa swallowed. 'I forgot you did that memory thing.' She looked at Catherine in fond astonishment. 'Yeah, those knives. I didn't realise, but one must have gone when the house was broken into and the doll arrived. Anyway, the cops bagged the remaining one when they did the initial search of the house. With a weapon and motive...' she let the sentence trail off and her hands gripped thin air.

For the first time in their friendship, Catherine thought she was about to see Melissa cry.

Catherine's look hardened, her forehead creasing, though she reached across the table and took Melissa's forearm. 'Well, that sucks.'

Catherine had been working on her understatements for some time.

'Yep.' Melissa let out a weak smile.

'Did you tell the cops about your intuition?'

'Yep.'

'Feel a bit stupid now?'

'Yep, yep.' Melissa repeated things occasionally, but only when they were important.

'So where were you last night?'

'Like I told them – I cast a circle in the backyard. It was equinox.'

'Can anyone verify that?'

'Magus. And the spirit of Ostara, who I worshipped with till about two. Then I had a smoke and watched *Buffy*.'

'I don't think spirits or familiars can stand up in court. Did you hear anything?'

'No. My sound system is pretty awesome.'

'A wheat sheaf. Would that have anything to do with your rite?'

'Wheat and ears of corn are part of the equinox ritual.'

'Did you tell the police that?'

Melissa paused. 'I did.'

'And did they tell you that...?'

'The dead girl was staring at one? Yes, they did, though only after I told them.'

'Don't say anything else without a lawyer.'

'They did offer me one, but I didn't think I needed one.'

'If this ever happens again, just assume you need a lawyer and don't say a bloody word until they're beside you.'

'Mum's the word.'

Catherine's brow furrowed slightly. 'What about that creepy bloke over the fence – would he have seen you?'

'He's at a *Star Wars* convention in Canberra.'

'Of course he is; where else would he be?'

Now Melissa did crumble, she buried her face into the back of her wrist, shaking almost imperceptibly. Again Catherine took her other wrist, gripping it tightly this time.

'Don't get ahead of yourself; you didn't kill anyone, right? This isn't Salem, no one's afraid of witches anymore.'

Melissa's voice was a whisper. 'I'll be fine. It's just been a big day.'

Gradually the shaking subsided. Melissa breathed deeply. 'I'm gonna go home. They'll be done by now. I'm gonna take a sleeping tablet and be unconscious for a while. Times like this I miss vodka.' She stood up quickly. As Catherine stood as well, Melissa gripped her shoulder.

'Thanks, babe. Nothing like being implicated in a murder to really ruin your day.'

It was when they embraced that Catherine looked out of the window. She froze, then forced herself to relax and as she let go of Melissa, she gave a smile. Just be reassuring.

She should have known that they might be watched. If an investigation was in play, it was procedure. She just wasn't ready to see him: Detective Kenneth Williams. She could only see his frame in the passenger seat of an unmarked car, but she knew who it was straight away, just as surely as she knew winter was cold and Stetsons were over-rated.

Melissa was already departing for her car and the unmarked was indicating to move into traffic. Catherine walked onto the road and stood between the traffic and the unmarked, blocking its path. Through the windscreen, she watched his face almost imperceptibly harden. He mouthed a word quietly to the driver. The car reversed back into the parking space and the engine died. Williams got out of the car. Hulking and middle aged, he wore his grey suit and tie as if he showered in them.

Catherine didn't move. 'Oh sorry, am I standing your way?' She looked momentarily at her feet. 'Shoot. Hey, you seem to have lost the sirens, have you been robbed?'

He looked at her for a full ten seconds; neither of them spoke. Then Williams ran his forefinger and thumb down either side of his face. The way he always did when he was trying to keep calm.

'You're standing in front of a police car, Catherine.'

'Sssshhhh.' She brought an exaggerated finger to her lips and then said in a stage whisper: 'I think you might be undercover.'

'You're not impressing me.'

Catherine returned to her usual voice, but did not move. 'You're investigating an innocent woman.'

'I don't think I need to tell you what I'm investigating, Catherine. How about you just get out of our way?'

'Moving pretty fast today. Melissa said you had the warrant by noon.'

His mouth creased. He breathed through his nose a second before he made a movement with his hand. Come closer, it said. They moved onto the footpath, standing close.

Williams spoke quietly: 'You wouldn't knowingly compromise an investigation. Why are you making a scene?'

'Just the shock of one of my friends being accused of a murder. It's the kind of thing I get riled about.'

'I don't know what you're talking about.'

Catherine smiled humourlessly. 'So two men from St Kilda Road are just hanging in Brunswick after a murder for what? Vietnamese food? Pork rolls?'

Suddenly his finger was pointed at her, his hand low, pointing towards her stomach and quivering.

'You gave up any right to question my methods a long time ago. I saw your name on the report. I'll be in touch when we need to ask you questions. Call your lawyer.' He started towards the car.

'If you're in charge, you're wasting your time on this. Melissa—'

He spun around, quicker than a man of his age should be able. 'Yeah, I'm in charge.' His face twitched. 'You're wasting my time. If she did it, tell her to confess. If she didn't, I'll work it out. But it looks bad.'

'So I should just trust you then?'

'You should just make a hat, or something.'

She took a detour on the way home, walking through her favourite park, to digest the day's events and the fact that she had let Williams have the last word. She looked through the leaves dancing in the trees and thought about hats that should have been made a week ago. The timing was terrible; with the spring racing carnival coming Catherine had an ever-growing list of work to do. It was typical of Melissa to get her involved during spring. Then she thought of the dead woman in the alley and suddenly there was nothing to feel irritated about.

The day had come, years earlier, when Catherine stopped actively pursuing mysteries, or as her mother put it, "stopped even miming the straight and narrow". After a car accident, she realised she had only so many summers on earth. The next day she stopped working for the police. Stopped living quietly in anticipation of the weekend, and made every day the day she looked forward to.

Williams hadn't taken it well. They had worked together indirectly for two years, and had become close. Catherine had made moves towards becoming "sworn". No longer a civilian on contract, but a policewoman. Catherine had expected him to be disappointed, but not betrayed. They had hardly spoken since that day. The last thing he had said to her was, 'You could have been a real copper.'

Her mum said she could have been a great lawyer. Her teachers said she could have been a leader. Her grandmother once told her she could marry a prime minister.

It's hard to disappoint people who believe in you, even when they come out with rubbish like that.

She had always been attracted to what other people avoided in humanity. To the extremes of what we did to one another. What she sometimes called the darkness. There are two ways to deal with that darkness: to immerse yourself in it, to the point where you mirrored it, or to sing so loud that the darkness was filled with life. Up until that point, her adult life was filled with working side by side with men like Williams, a man who pushed against the darkness so much it was all he knew.

There were other ways to make a living, other ways to help people. She had money, passed on by a successful family, which made the change financially possible. Leaving the police wasn't denying the darkness; it was just her way of pushing against it without becoming it.

That was why she made hats and drank until the small hours. That was why she danced until dawn. It wasn't perfect, she knew she should make more hats and drink less, but it was life, a noisy, throbbing life.

She also knew that these things would occasionally find her, as they usually did those who can't live quietly. So the deal came: follow beauty, until you must follow horror. When that time comes, follow horror until it is understood, and do it smiling.

She did this because she could, and it had saved lives.

Here she was again, working through the darkness. The case against Melissa wasn't watertight, though the knife, the proximity and the revenge motive did, as Williams put it, "look bad". Catherine was sure that Melissa, even if she were remanded, would deal with prison well and probably change the path of many a fallen woman. Catherine, however, was far too selfish for such fine thoughts and wanted to keep Melissa close to her own slow, graceful descent. If life was a vortex, one should keep good company.

The text message she sent was brief, but its meaning would be ascertained. 'Private browsing invite to Ms Brittany Houden, many new styles in from Paris and an intriguing local sensation. Please advise a suitable time for Brunswick Studio. CK'

Cassandra had only met Melissa the once, at the Victorian Civil and Appeals Tribunal. That was all it took. Cassandra had been representing Jewel Real Estate as the property manager for a flat that Melissa had left. When Melissa had arrived at the flat she had bought a large purple rug to stop her cat from ruining the carpet. When she left she found that same rug had left a purple stain on the floor that no amount of steam cleaning could redeem. The landlord argued that the carpet had been ruined, Melissa counter-argued the carpet must have been useless to begin with and offered $200 compensation. The real estate agency took the $200 and then demanded $400 more. Melissa took the issue to VCAT for the $400 owing; and she walked out owing $800. Cassandra had argued passionately for the firm and the landlord. Melissa took it personally and when the appeal failed she took her case to the fourth estate.

Since arriving home Catherine had only stopped to make tea before poring over the CV of the deceased on the internet. A young, aspiring realtor, she had a double degree in business studies and feminism and had twice won the Real Estate Institute of Victoria property manager of the year award. Her biography on the estate agent's website painted the picture of a motivated and empathetic property manager who had been a former debating champion and loved working at Jewel. Her photo stared back at Catherine from the screen. She was beautiful, with a winning smile, large dark eyes and a face that had benefitted from the gene pools of at least two continents. The photo showed a bright young professional in a demanding job with a long future she should have been able to look forward to. Fast forward to this morning, dead from violence. Even if Catherine's friend wasn't suspected, she would have wanted to help on this case.

Cassandra Pierce's only other hit on the internet was the article in Catherine's own community newspaper, *The Brunswick Express*. The *Express* was a free weekly full of ads and a smattering of community news.

Catherine re-read the article about Melissa placing a curse on Jewel Real Estate, and in particular Cassandra.

Local musician and "magical practitioner" Melissa Zamansky has taken her real estate dispute into the realm of the spiritual by placing a curse on Jewel Real Estate. A separate hex was placed on her former property manager Cassandra Pierce. Melissa Zamansky has taken the unusual step after losing a dispute raised in the Victorian Civil and Appeal Tribunal last month. Zamansky told the Express that while she was defeated in the tribunal, she had other means at her disposal. 'Just because Cassandra has won in the tribunal does not mean she is safe from my power,' Zamansky said.

Catherine rolled her eyes and reminded herself what a good friend Melissa was when she wasn't trying to be famous. Catherine personally thought that it was ridiculous that Melissa hadn't spent her wrath on the seller of the purple rug. She could imagine that Melissa, having lost face and money at VCAT, would have tried to console herself with a bit of publicity. As fun as she was, it was exactly the kind of idiocy that seemed to occur periodically to her.

Jewel Real Estate seemed a good place for enemies, and Catherine needed to see who else would want ill to come to Cassandra.

'Jewel Real Estate; you're speaking with Jane.'

'Jane, hi. My name's Catherine Kint; I've been expecting a call from Cassandra Pierce, regarding the shower pressure in my unit.' Catherine had decided to keep it simple.

'Ah, Cassandra.' Jane's voice caught in her throat upon exhalation.

'Is she there?' Catherine hated this part; it went against all her notions of human kindness.

'No… she's dead.' Her voice was apologetic.

'Oh.' Catherine's fingers fluttered as she counted to two. 'I'm sorry.'

'Thank you,' Jane's voice gained assurance as she reverted to a script. 'Due to this sudden, tragic event we're running a little behind. Most of Cassandra's work will be picked up by Marcus Frawley; I could put you through to him if you'd like.'

'Will Marcus be across the issues?'

'He and Cassandra worked very closely, I'm sure he could help.'

'No, it's OK. I'll call next week, you must all be devastated.'

'Yes, it's horrible, such a tragedy.'

Twenty minutes later Catherine was staring across Sydney Road at Jewel Real Estate. Hipsters, trams and Indian mynah birds moved across an inconspicuous grey building illuminated by spring sunshine.

Catherine strode in and smiled her best Girl Guides smile.

'Hi, I'm Catherine. I'm here to see Marcus Frawley.'

A short, thin man walked into the front office, as if on cue. His angular face was set off by his dark hair in a coif and he had a golden stud in his left ear. He looked to Catherine's shoes and slowly back to her face, before twitching his head in a newsreader's salute that made his hair wiggle. 'I'm Marcus.'

'Hi, Marcus. I'm sorry to hear of your loss.'

'Yes, a tragedy.' He took her hand in a loose grip, that indicated he would kiss it but for a deft twist of Catherine's wrist.

'My name is Catherine Kint. Do you have a minute?'

Marcus' confidence didn't drop for a second. 'Of course,' his arm pointed in an easterly direction, 'I'm over there.'

Seated in his street-facing office, Catherine watched as he closed the door, muting the sounds of phones and office chatter. Marcus turned and smiled as if he'd been waiting for this moment his whole life.

'Do you have a property with us, Catherine?'

'No, I'm not really here about property.'

'So why are you here then, Catherine Kint?' he said playfully.

'I'm a person with an interest in Cassandra. A friend of mine is under suspicion of her murder. I know this to be improbable and I thought you might be able to help me.' It was blunt, she knew, but she could also bet both her great-grandmothers' earrings that Marcus thought of himself as a man of the world, in the weary way that many real estate people did.

'Why me?'

'Just because you worked closely with her. I won't waste much of your time. I imagine you can guess what I want to know. Do you know who she associated with? Did she have any enemies?'

He sat at his desk and stroked his hair with his fingers. 'I told all this to the police. No enemies, coupla hundred friends, probably a dozen lovers,' he winked at this point. 'Outside the office I hardly knew her.'

'Was she popular around the office?'

He paused for a second, put his hands together as if praying. 'She was good at the job. No question,' he shrugged. 'She knew it, which didn't always endear her, but now is not the time for that.'

'Any trouble with clients?'

'Nothing worth mentioning.'

'What about friends? If I wanted to know a bit more about her, who would I talk to?'

Marcus lent back in his chair, left eyebrow raised. 'Am I not helpful enough?'

Catherine became slightly nauseous. All she could think for an awful second was about the real likelihood of this man having a Japanese character tattooed on his back. She smiled with no teeth.

'I'm extremely grateful to you for your assistance. Perhaps you could tell me about the past few weeks – has Cassandra acted any differently? Has she seemed stressed?'

He looked down for a second, as if to something in the drawers of his desk and then looked up quickly. 'I'm sorry, Catherine,' he said, then laughed a little. 'Look I don't want it getting round that I don't like beautiful women coming to my office, but I really don't have time for this, huh? Someone died, it's awful, but someone has to do the work, and that's me. If you'd like to do dinner or something, I'd be happy to talk later.'

No chance. Catherine felt sure Melissa would understand.

'I have some experience in this, Marcus. Usually there's a reason for murder. People could be in danger. Thanks though, I won't take more of your time.' She started getting out of her chair.

The brush-off hit home, but only for a second. His professional smile was right back.

'Why don't you go talk with her boyfriend?'

For the first time Catherine noticed he was sweating, despite the air-conditioned office.

Catherine paused with her pen over her notebook. 'What's his name?'

Marcus stared at her for a second, then gave a small smile. 'Asher is his name. I assure you he knows her better and almost certainly has more time than me. Hey, just curious. How do you know your friend didn't do it?'

'I know her.'

Marcus smiled, an open palm gesturing towards the door. 'I just hope it all gets sorted out.'

'Could you tell me Cassandra's boyfriend's full name?'

Marcus touched his eyebrow. 'Marr. Asher Marr. He's a guru, or yogi or something.' He was speaking quickly. 'I hardly ever met him.'

'Thanks.'

She stepped back into the office. A flurry of people in dark clothes were moving quickly against an off-white back drop. On a far wall Cassandra, holding an award, stared out from a framed photo. Catherine knew they were busy, but it bothered her that none of them seemed to notice.

Asher Marr had only one listing in the phone book, at least according to her phone's internet browser. He wasn't listed as a guru or a yoga teacher. This meant little aside from surprise that there was one listed at all. Many people, especially of a spiritualist bent, didn't want to be contactable. At least in the conventional, "My name is in the phone book" kind of way. Catherine was once told by a UFO enthusiast this was because it made them easier to be found by the Government. This had tickled her, as it indicated that some people actually thought the best tool the Government had to keep tabs on people was the white pages. It was these rambling thoughts; the kind which occasionally plagued her when she was hungry, that occupied her grey matter when she dialled the number of Asher Marr.

A sitar sounded on the line, followed by the recording of a male voice: 'Welcome to the Shining Way. We will be with you when we can; please leave a message.'

Once she heard the sitar she assumed the voice would be American, but the pleasant male voice spoke with an accent that was pure Melbourne.

'This is Catherine; please show me the way.' With that she left her number and started walking to the address listed in the phone book.

The Shining Way – A Guided Life, was run out of a new age clothing shop a block from Sydney Road. Catherine must have passed it a million times, but had never once ventured in. On one side was the back of one of the warehouses that still dominated patches of Brunswick and on the other was a cut-price bicycle repair joint which catered to the thousands of cyclists who darted up the Upfield train line's bike path.

The Shining Way shop had a "Closed" sign, but Catherine believed that signs were there to be interpreted, and so to her it conveyed "Closed to anyone who wants to discuss Pisces ascending, but open to seekers of truth, enlightenment and who killed the girl", so she proceeded to knock. She was not at all surprised when she heard some movement inside or when, four minutes later, the door opened.

He was around thirty, about six foot, and sharply handsome. He had piercing blue eyes framed by wavy dark hair that rested on high cheekbones rarely seen outside of magazines. He either had a tan or was of an ethnicity that gave the effect of one year round. He gave a half smile. 'Hello?'

'Hello. Are you Asher?'

He paused, staring intently. 'I am.'

'I'm Catherine. I'm terribly sorry about Cassandra. I was wondering if you could help me.'

In this Catherine used two of her favourite approaches: firstly, she was direct, which people either loved or hated; secondly, she wasn't launching into an interrogation but simply asking for help. It usually worked well, especially with men.

'Are you a journalist?' He continued to peer at her as if she were a new type of human he hadn't encountered before. This apparent appreciation combined very pleasantly with his angular jaw.

'No – I'm Catherine.' She looked down at herself, as if to make sure, and smiled her most unassuming smile. She could smell incense from the shop wafting around her. Asher returned the grin, touching the side of his face as if he had forgotten what smiling was.

'So you are. Would you like to…'

A second man appeared at the door, a version of Asher, but with wider features; broader shoulders, and a scowl. He gave the feeling of a factory second.

'What?'

The question was spat out and accompanied by a look of menace. Catherine wondered if he were stoned.

Asher laid a hand on his shoulder, but it was shrugged it off. Asher put it back on his brother's shoulder, as if pulling him back from a fight.

'Sorry. My brother, Shiloh.'

Catherine decided the shop's incense was affecting her brain, because she found herself comparing the brothers' energies. Shiloh also had olive skin and dark hair (though his was longer, a regrettable decision), but he pulsed with tension. Asher, meanwhile, seemed unperturbed by his brother's reaction. Maybe only Asher was on the path to peace; maybe, in this time of turmoil, Shiloh's aura was affected by the second star of Orion. Maybe years of unfavourable comparison to his handsome brother had eroded Shiloh's self-esteem and in turn, his manners. Or maybe, as was sometimes the case, one brother was simply a jerk. Catherine brought herself back to the task at hand.

'Hello, Shiloh. I was asking if Asher could help me.'

'There's no business at this time,' Shiloh grunted, staring at his brother, who ignored him. 'Death in the family.' He started pulling Asher into the doorway. Asher resisted, pushing past his brother's hand.

'Hey, give her a sec.'

Catherine took a step towards Asher. 'I wanted to talk to you about Cassandra.'

Shiloh pulled Asher's arm. He turned to Catherine. 'Go!'

As he pulled Asher out of the doorway, Catherine noticed several things:

a) Shiloh's skin was tanned. A pale band on his little finger suggested he had recently lost or stopped wearing a ring.

b) The door was made of a thick hardwood that seemed excessive by modern standards.

c) Her foot was in imminent danger of being crushed by said door.

Asher gave a resigned sigh and waved a small apology or goodbye to Catherine. Even as the door slammed he didn't break eye contact with her.

In the silence that followed, Catherine became aware that she was standing on Henry Street facing a closed door and that the hair on the back of her neck was on end. She felt the urge to skip.

No one should feel this excited when a door slams on them.

Everyone should feel this excited about a handsome man at least every six months. It had been longer. This should be good.

The sun was certainly shining over the yardarm by the time Catherine had moved back to her own neck of Brunswick. Melissa could be helped no further until tomorrow. This was the point of the day where she would go home, eat vegetarian super-foods and spend the evening working. Poring over the backlog of broad brims, pillboxes and crowns that had taken a number and waited all day. She would listen to political podcasts and drink vast quantities of soda water. Then she would do her BAS statements and call her mother. Or she could go to the pub.

As she crossed the threshold of the Glasgow Palace, Catherine shed herself of her metaphorical deerstalker and allowed herself a minute to think about gin. The French say the best part of an affair is going up the stairs; Catherine believed one of the best things about gin was the anticipation.

Although nothing seems boring to someone enjoying their first two gins of the evening, news from the pub was, all things considered, reasonably interesting. Boris had mostly recovered from the trauma and was deflecting the attention his brush with crime had brought upon him. The outrage that such a terrible crime could occur here or anywhere brought the conversation round to the historical mistreatment of women from Anne Boleyn through to Yoko Ono. Catherine felt a glow not entirely caused by gin towards the raconteurs, failed academics and wasted wits that lurked in this rather tasteful den of iniquity.

Catherine took a second to watch her friend pour her gin without asking what she wanted. A good man behind the bar is a thing to be treasured, Catherine had told him just that on the one or two occasions when she came as close to slurring as a lady does. Despite his best attempts, and a somewhat scruffy beard, Boris was a good man. In a quiet nook, they went over the day's events.

'I just can't get over the way she was staring.'

'Not exactly, Boris. She was dead. But, yes, it was nonetheless a good impersonation of staring.'

'So you don't think she was fixated by something when she was killed?'

'She might have been, I can't imagine. At any rate, I draw the line at saying she was staring. Staring is a verb and verbs are doing things and things are not done by dead people.'

'Well put. Another?'

'I think it's best.'

'Y'know,' Boris began as he chopped the lemon, 'a bloke was telling me about some chemical that is released into your bloodstream only twice in your life, as you're born and as you die. He said he had a drug that released it and that it was amazing.'

'Tempted?'

'A little. You?'

'No. As interested as I am in the shamanic, I think that if it's only released twice then we must only have a certain store of it, which presumably we'll need at some stage. Like serotonin – as we get older we have less, which explains the bad moods of some elderly people and their tendency towards conservatism.'

'Serotonin is the stuff ecstasy unleashes, right?'

'Yes, which means in another forty years, when the rave generation retires, we're in for a bad time. Imagine: a generation of former pill-heads living out their last decades in a permanent moody Tuesday funk.'

'Bad grandparents.'

'The worst.'

'A shame. I loved my Granny,' Boris said.

'She ever get grumpy with you?'

'Only when I used her false teeth.'

'What did you use them for?'

'Her cat. I used them as extra teeth so I could bite it back extra hard. That moggy was a serious piece of work.'

'It probably did too much E as a kitten.'

Boris was called to pour more beers, leaving Catherine to muse on recent events. What would cause someone to leave a doll in a house and kill someone behind the house weeks later? Melissa's doll and Cassandra's death seemed too much of coincidence.

The further mystery was how the hell the police thought Melissa, a wiry but tiny woman, could have overpowered and slit the throat of the taller, heavier Cassandra. Catherine counted the bottles on the top shelf in Japanese and then counted backwards in Russian. She had found this a good way of distracting her brain while her guts formulated a plan.

'Boris, what are you doing tomorrow?'

'Day off. Taking myself to the movies – wanna come?'

'I want to stop you going. How would you like some excitement in your life?'

'Oh Catherine, you speak seven languages, I speak Klingon. You went to regattas growing up, I thought they were pasta. Should we really take our relationship further?'

Catherine smiled her smile that she reserved only for Boris; it was his consolation prize.

'Nothing so athletic, I hope. I want you to follow a man around, a real estate agent.'

'Just follow?'

'Yes, you don't even have to talk to him. I had that pleasure today. I just want to make sure he didn't kill Cassandra. I don't think he did, but he's a sleaze and you know…' Her hands moved as if she were juggling slow moving balls over her drink.

'Most people who kill others are sleazy?'

'Well it's not an exact science, but yes. I'll provide your usual retainer.'

'My landlord will thank you. What's his name?'

'Marcus Frawley. He worked with Cassandra at Jewel Real Estate.'

'What does he look like?'

'Like a man who shines his shoes twice a week and kisses his own picture before going to work each day.'

'So I'll look for a lower level real estate dude then.'

'He has a rockabilly look, if that helps, and an earring.'

'I'm sure I'll work it out.'

3

It's a good day when you don't notice people not noticing you.
~ Catherine Kint

A new day dawned, finding Boris at his side job of taking on errands for Catherine. It was seasonal work, only happening when Catherine found herself involved with a case, but it paid better than bar work. It had an air of derring-do, despite the fact that it was rarely daring and often involved doing nothing at all. He was seated at an outside table at a Sydney Road cafe, had read the morning papers, and drained his fourth long black. To be precise, he was sitting across the road from Jewel Real Estate, having read all about Marcus Frawley on their website.

Marcus was a rental superstar who had been with Jewel for the past ten years. He liked the real estate lifestyle, Elvis, true crime books and fast cars. Boris had only the faintest clue of what "the real estate lifestyle" was, but he assumed that it involved early mornings and late nights talking about houses. The idea made him shiver.

Boris was betting on Frawley being a local boy, but still assumed he would drive. A friend once told him that people in real estate rent expensive cars to seem more successful, and he thought of that any time he hated being a barman. Boris was surprised when he saw Frawley using public transport, but yet, sure enough, the 8.38am tram disgorged him like an olive-green caterpillar displeased with its lunch. Frawley bounded off the tram like he was jumping onto a stage. He walked with a slight swagger. He was exactly as Catherine had described.

Boris, who had never strutted sober in his life, took an instant dislike to him.

He kept his eyes fixed in the middle distance as his quarry walked past him into the cafe and ordered a coffee. Through the open windows Boris listened to Frawley's voice, all faux affability; he twice checked with the barista as to his coffee's place in the queue. Clearly, the man was a genuine prick.

Ten minutes later Frawley was tucked into his office and Boris was wondering if the day would pass with him shooting coffees he didn't want. He decided to perform some background checks. Heading into the cafe, he flashed his pearlies at the now relaxed, and rather pretty, barista.

'That bloke who just left, with the trench coat and the dark hair – is he famous? I'm sure I've seen him somewhere.'

The girl looked puzzled. 'Marcus? No. Though he always seems in a hurry, so he could be important.' She wiped the inside of the coffee head, causing her tattooed arms to flap like she was doing the chicken dance. 'He doesn't chat much and I don't mind that.'

Boris smiled wanly; he was always good with a hint. He left her and went back to his seat, wondering if girls would like him more if he got one of those earlobe stretcher rings.

At 10.14am Frawley was spotted again, this time outside the office trying to hail a taxi. Boris bolted his coffee and dumped a twenty on the table. He had parked his old Ford Laser around the corner and he reached it as only an over-caffeinated barman can, dancing around a man walking his dog, a niqab-wearing woman with a child in a stroller, and a deciduous tree. He was nimble as a jungle cat, until he smacked the car door into his shin as he opened it. His eyes were still watering as he turned the keys in the ignition and eased towards Sydney Road. He was relieved to find Frawley still in view, climbing into a north-facing taxi.

Boris found a gap in the traffic just a few cars behind. After five minutes of uneventful driving, the taxi stopped outside a local primary school. Frawley walked across the road to a block of yellow-brick flats. Boris parked as far from the school as he could without losing sight of the gate. This changed the rules somewhat. Waiting patiently in a cafe is one thing – many law-abiding people do that every day. Waiting outside a primary school when you have no children of your own can injure one's reputation as a gentleman.

After forty minutes, Boris had recorded in his notebook:

10.32: Frawley meets large man and enters flats, possibly work related.

10.35: F and X return outside, X gesturing to ivy growing up the building. F takes photos. Also possibly work related.

10.37: F and X shake hands and X departs. F knocks on further door and converses with occupant. Looks like general real estate business. Must ask Catherine for pay rise.

10.41: F takes mobile phone call, seems animated. Possibly MURDER related.

10.55: F makes phone call.

10.59: F steps into taxi, heads south.

This was hardly Woodward and Bernstein, thought Boris. He prepared himself for further caffeinated monotony as Frawley's taxi departed.

Or so he thought. Back at Sydney Road the taxi indicated and swerved to the curb. Boris passed and took the next parking space he could find. Frawley alighted and the taxi moved on, passing Boris' parked car and heading north. Boris watched Frawley in his rear-view mirror. Frawley was on his mobile. He was standing outside a pokies joint just a few blocks from the Glasgow Palace. The man's swagger was gone and he hunched into himself. There were a few ugly men in the pub windows, staring at their drinks. Boris thought they all looked guilty. It fit with Catherine's great theory number three: everyone has a guilty conscience. Whatever Frawley was talking about, he wasn't having a good day.

Stepping out of the car, Boris made a show of locking up and looking in the back for something he'd forgotten, and then strode down the street. Frawley turned away from his approach, shielding his words, but that only made them louder once Boris had passed him.

'No one wants it to go down like that – do you think I'm stupid?'

Boris slowed and browsed a junk shop's footpath display, admiring the magnificent array of plastic roses.

'No, no, no, not your turf – it's gone too far for that. My office, 6pm tomorrow.'

Boris examined a plastic rose as if he had just found the face of Jesus in it.

'Oh yes, I'm sure you're following me all the time. You just see what happens.' Boris chanced a glance in the reflection of the shop window. Frawley wasn't talking to him. He had hung up the phone and stared down the street towards Jewel Real Estate. He ran a hand through his coif and turned his face to the pub. He checked the time on his phone and marched in. For the first time Boris felt he understood the man; some days you just need a beer at 11.30.

Boris put down the miracle rose, counted to thirty-five, and followed. It was a barn of a place: flashing lights, big televisions, pumping music and the atmosphere of a morgue. Frawley had a pot of dark ale and headed to sit in the corner, furthest from the window. Simply to fit in, taking no pleasure in his job at all, Boris ordered a pot of beer and moved to a window table. Idly staring at a greyhound race being won by a dog called Fingers, Boris wondered if it was a sign, and then chided himself. He was haunted by the memory of the corpse, but that was no excuse for finding a greyhound's name mystical.

Movement in the pub's corner awoke him from his morbid thoughts. Frawley's pot had stopped halfway to his mouth, his face was flushed and not from the drink. Boris followed the man's stare and saw a tall man with dark hair pulled back from his face in a loose ponytail. He wore a black top with a blue, sleeveless jacket over it, hot for spring, with dark jeans and better shoes than Boris could afford. The man smiled carnivorously at Frawley and gestured with his hands like a magician revealing the trick – surprise, I'm over here. The most unnerving thing was, after he stopped glaring at Frawley, he turned straight to Boris. He had the look of a man who'd keep a dog hungry.

Boris looked at the stranger's potent hands and felt a small wave crash somewhere in the pit of his stomach. Fight and flight instincts rushed through him without either winning, so he adopted a glazed expression. He watched traffic on the street; as all the brave lines from a hundred movies slipped harmlessly through his head. He felt, more than saw, the stranger's gaze slide over to Frawley.

Frawley walked quickly towards the stranger and the door. He pushed his shoulder into the stranger's chest, an act of defiance to offset the fact that he was trying to run away, fast. The taller man didn't reel but his arm shot out and tapped Frawley on the back of the head. Frawley kept moving towards the door, but the other man stood still. Boris sensed the stranger's eyes on him. He was faced with the choice of continuing his implausible absent staring trick, or squaring his shoulders and enquiring if the bloke had a problem.

When he turned back a moment later the man had gone. Boris grabbed his beer and found it strangely empty. On a scale of one to ten, he felt rattled. As ever in such situations, he knew that Indiana Jones would have handled it better.

Boris couldn't see any sign of the pair on the street outside. He tried the alleyway by the side of the pub, and saw a man walking away with a fast, easy stride. Boris' first instinct was to chase, and his second, to not make it so obvious that he was doing so. Bolting down alleys in broad daylight didn't seem like part of a good day's quiet surveillance.

He decided instead to walk south, in the assumed direction of Frawley. He mused on what was known: someone, possibly the tall stranger or someone known to that pony-tailed scaremonger, intimidated Frawley. The realtor did not think he was being followed until he realised he was. Unfortunately, that meant that the follower might also have known that Boris was following Frawley, too. Worse, that the incident in the pub would mean that if Boris turned up at the coffee shop again, Frawley would almost certainly spot him straight away as the beer-drinking, plastic-flower enthusiast.

Still, if Frawley was already frightened, maybe Boris could shake something out of him. Unless the altercation in the pub had nothing to do with Cassandra Pierce's death, and Boris might just be wasting his own time, Catherine's money in following a third-rate real estate agent. For all he knew, Frawley and the tall bloke were lovers; maybe they even liked plastic flowers. So many unknowns.

Boris wrestled with this moment of doubt, then, because he didn't have another plan, kept walking. The day flowed windy around him. Tradies were breaking for lunch; mums with prams moved around and past him looking tired and alive. There was still no sign of Frawley or the stranger. As a tram rattled past, Boris thought he caught a flash of light, but saw nothing past the tinted windows and the smiling face of Bert Newton.

He headed back to the same outdoor table he sat at earlier. While he'd probably already been identified he decided that Frawley didn't seem like the cop-calling type. He ordered a beer and watched people file in and out of the Jewel Real Estate office. He was contemplating calling Catherine when the waitress arrived with his frosty and rather welcome VB. As he smiled and thanked her, she gestured under his table, 'You drop those?'

Boris looked under his seat. He found two flat objects, not dropped by him. One was a Polaroid of him taken ten minutes earlier; the other was the drawing of a hand with three fingers missing.

4

Ingenious is the invisible thing that makes you move towards it.
~ Melissa Zamansky

Catherine had been musing on the benefits of black witchcraft earlier that morning. If you had a run-in with a witch before 10am, it meant that the day could only improve from there, she decided. It had been eight minutes to ten, precisely, when a middle aged woman approached her on the footpath near her local grocery store. The woman was muttering in the way of the irritatingly insane and, not being in the mood for a talk on the wild side, Catherine had checked her watch to avoid eye contact. This was how she was so sure it was eight minutes to ten when this woman yelled: 'Ye who try to protect the wicked shall be burned by flowers.'

This gave Catherine pause for thought, because it is not every day one is insulted in an entirely new and exciting fashion. She turned to this taunting woman with such quaint phrasing.

'Good morning. Kindly tell me what it is you want or please stop sharing my oxygen.'

'You would protect her.'

The woman's voice was shrill, her grey eyes indignant and wide, dominating a face framed by her shock of brown hair. It was an amazing voice, but it was the woman's nose that really stood out; part ski jump, part battering ram, it was the kind of nose that either built character or destroyed its owner. It was an occupation-specific nose, if one was born with it, people didn't ask what you wanted to be when you grew up, they just knew it was either perfumery or witchcraft.

'If you mean my cat,' said Catherine, gesturing with the bag of hair-ball control cat food she had just purchased, 'then yes, that's correct. But I don't think you mean Minty, so I'm going to ask you a question now. Are you a witch?'

'You dare call me a witch?' The voice was full and would have been convincing if she hadn't spent a full second and a half on each word while pointing at Catherine like Banquo's ghost. Sadly for this witch-in-denial, Catherine had always harboured a long and passionate hatred of pantomime and thus was not in the mood for further discussion. The lights turned green and on she walked.

But the witch kept pace with Catherine, who ignored her and counted to twenty under her breath. Catherine had done so in English, Spanish, Hebrew and Japanese before the woman began her accusations again.

'You will see the evils in the power of the hand, within the moves of foul air and the cut fingers of a madman, yet you protect those that should burn and thus you have allowed yourself to be corrupted by flowers.'

Catherine stopped and turned. 'Do you know Melissa, and if you do, what do you want?' She was fierce when angry, and while she could put up with weirdoes – and even endure pantomime – she had not forgotten Melissa was in the frame for a long stretch in a cell.

The witch waved her hands like she was wearing puppets.

'Save yourself; she does not deserve your pity.'

'Do you mean Cassandra? What do you know?' Catherine leaned towards the woman, who raised a chin in defiance.

'I'm talking about the charlatan sorceress.'

'If you're talking about Mel, she does deserve pity, because she is being investigated for murder and that's a big deal in this dimension. Now I'm going to ask again, just once more, before I shower you with nutritious organic treats for felines: what do you want?'

The witch looked pained. 'She does not deserve,' she said unhappily. She made a gesture as though trying to catch a mosquito, then pushed this imaginary insect towards Catherine, before she convulsed and threw up into the gutter.

Catherine melted from stony to pitying. The witch was bent almost double, her spit mingling with her breakfast in the gutter. Catherine hoped it would rain soon. She leaned in to touch the woman's shoulder but the woman straightened and moved backwards. Silently, she wiped her mouth, staring as if Catherine were the risen dead. She stumbled away double quick, slowing only when she backed into a group of black-clad Greek grandmothers who gestured their wards against the evil eye at her retreating form.

'Pathological,' Catherine muttered. She would have to tell Melissa about this. It made sense that Melissa would have some rivals in the magical subculture, but still that lady was a joke. A scary witch, Catherine decided, a truly powerful one, would likely not look like a witch, not talk like a witch, and would probably work five days a week for UNICEF or Halliburton.

As she passed the Glasgow Palace and turned the corner for home, a funny thing happened.

As a lady, she liked to know the comings and goings of any breathing being that entered her underpants. She was embarrassed to note that some insect had obviously penetrated her defences, because her left buttock had begun to itch in a most undesired way. Catherine could feel her neck muscles tense with the effort to keep her composure. With a desperate glance both ways she lowered her hand to dislodge whatever insect had bitten her, but found nothing. The itch got worse, and her skin became hot. In order to maintain decorum, Catherine imagined herself in a far-off place and quickened her step. She power-walked to her flat while her mind took her to the southern hemisphere of Pluto. She imagined the dark cliffs and expanses barely illuminated by the distant sun. She imagined the mix of nitrogen and methane that she would breathe, calculated how many socks she would need to pack to avoid frost bite. She concentrated on the image of the sun staring coolly out towards her through space. She knew about that sun, she would give it a name, and the name was Itchy Itchy Itchy. She could only count how many steps to her door: twenty, thirty, itchy paces.

Up the stairs and inside her flat Catherine scratched like a digging dog. It was incredible, but the scratching gave only the slightest relief. Ice did little, aloe vera dulled it for a second, gin helped only if taken orally. In desperation she remembered an old wives' tale and found herself, for the first time in her life, rubbing toothpaste on to her buttocks. The itch somehow intensified, and Catherine heard her own voice call out – and then it was gone.

Making a sound that was half cry and half sigh, Catherine fell on to the bathroom floor and found herself snuggling into her bathmat. It was thick and shaggy and luxurious and smelt sweetly of skin and lavender. She lay there for a full two minutes, revelling in the perfect moment. Fancy restaurants are lovely, sunsets and babies have their place, but true bliss only comes when your arse stops burning. It was one of the most pleasant moments Catherine had experienced in some time.

When she felt that she had spent enough time staring blissfully at the bathroom ceiling, Catherine decided to risk a shower. She stood up and craned back over her shoulder into the mirror. What she saw surprised her. Her fingers had raked her skin and given the impression that she had had a fight with a very short jaguar. This was to be expected; pale skin gets ravaged easily. Less expected was the vermillion mark where the itch had been. It looked like a lily.

Catherine mouthed the ancient voodoo curse she had learned while backpacking through the Caribbean. She recalled the rather flamboyant hand movement the witch had performed before vomiting.

As a young girl Catherine had been fascinated with birthmarks, and had wished for her own mark of distinction. She'd been disappointed when her mother informed her that she'd had one once, a small red dot on the side of her head, but it had disappeared not long after her second birthday. Perhaps she should be grateful, she mused, for this floral display on her otherwise flawless – she was told – derriere. Gratitude was not forthcoming, however, especially after two minutes in the shower when the itch crept back and gradually increased to the point where Catherine was again applying Colgate Enamel Protect to a place she had never assumed would require enamel protection.

Her phone distracted her. It was Melissa.

'Hey babe. How's it going?'

'I've had better mornings, but I'm hardly going to complain to you at this juncture. Any news?'

'I've been interviewed by police for the past three hours. They came in the early morning. They really want to know what I did with that poor girl's fingers. I'd love to help them, but no matter how intriguing the questions, I have no bloody idea. They must think I'm a nut they can crack eventually.'

'Just be truthful. Did you get a lawyer?'

'Lovely young lady, all of twenty-five, but she's smart.'

'Who's interviewing you?'

'Older guy called Williams; know him?'

'Yes I do.' Catherine exhaled. 'Talk about hard nuts to crack.'

'They haven't arrested me though. That's good, right?'

'Yeah, they won't arrest you. Hey, I think I got cursed this morning. Do you know a skinny woman of about forty who doesn't like you much? Does the whole wicked westie thing like she's in a kids' show?'

'Big nose?'

'That's her.'

'That's Alice. She's a pain in the arse – literally – and she never liked me. Said I was phony because I smoke tobacco instead of fish heads or whatever she uses shamanically. Do you have a flower on your bum?'

Catherine paused. 'Yes.'

'Only thing she can do. She's probably just pissed off about my publicity.'

'What publicity? You haven't been charged.'

'Honey, I was famous even before this.'

'Ye gods. I'll check you out when I get my fan mags.'

'I didn't kill the girl,' Melissa added helpfully.

'I know that. Think Alice might have?'

'No. She's annoying but she's not a killer.'

'There was a wheat sheaf at the murder scene; it was solstice and you didn't do it. I think I should check Alice out. Where would I find her?'

'Good luck. She drifts.'

'Any leads?'

'Try the halfway house on Stewart Street.'

'Can she fix this flower on my arse?'

'Don't worry, it's temporary. Try toothpaste.'

Catherine groaned and got back to business. 'I've got my man following one of Cassandra's colleagues, and I met her boyfriend's brother Shiloh. He was very hostile.'

'Brother of Asher?'

Catherine found herself smiling at the thought of him. 'Yeah, how did you know?'

'Famous family. Hey I gotta go; call you tomorrow.'

With that she was gone. Catherine was left wondering three things. First, how was Asher's family famous? Second, why was she enjoying the thought of seeing Asher so much? And third, who could help her find Cassandra's killer?

5

Wise men don't talk much. Shame, really.
~ Nealamber Singh

Nealamber Singh was one of nature's true happy chappies. Catherine had met him years ago at a charity ball when Neal offered to help her out of a window during a speech that was best described as tantric. Five minutes later, as they shared their disdain for the gratuitously virtuous, Neal had offered to be Catherine's connection to the internet. Catherine thought this a grand idea. She hadn't touched a computer since university, and had little desire to. She thought that Google was a cricketing term and Yahoo was a person who conversed with Jesus.

But at some point she knew computers were inevitable and she learned to download, upload and reboot. Although she could now Firefoxtrot across the web, Neal was still a port of call if Catherine needed help. He was very handy with a gentle hack at protected files if the cause was just.

Today, however, in Neal's spacious one-room bungalow, Catherine was finding it difficult to relax. She alternated between pacing and sitting under the strain of the recently cursed. Neal sat before two large computer screens, assorted wires, cables and magazines that on further inspection were featuring mostly wires and cables. Neal was very good at many things, and he certainly took the pain out of fact-checking, lead-finding, and reading up on where new restaurants were opening. He made his living selling audio education programs to children in China, despite having not a musical bone in his solid body.

He looked, as ever, like a serene librarian, with a large contented face and somewhat lopsided grin. Neal always appeared to have been recently woken from a slumber by a favourite grandchild; but he was only twenty-eight and had not seen his fiancée in three years. Neal had assured Catherine that the lovely June, his intended, was perfectly happy with a long engagement and regular Skype dates while she finished her medical degree in Bangalore. Catherine had always suspected that once June arrived it would end Neal's penchant for knitted maroon vests worn over very stiff collars. For a man obsessed with modern technology, his fashion was stuck firmly in 1947.

'Would you like more tea, Catherine? Do you need something stronger?'

'No, I'm fine with tea.'

'You seem jumpy.'

Catherine stopped pacing. While she adored Neal, her new lower body adornment was a secret she would rather keep. 'I'm full of concern for the result of the pending state election.'

'Your liberal soul will only bring you angst and the world will turn just as greedily.'

'Did your grandmother tell you that?'

'God rest her sweet soul.'

'Just be so good as to find anything in Cassandra Pierce's history that touched on magic, dolls, wheat or anything that mentions the names Asher Marr or Shiloh Marr.'

'Magic dolls, Asher, Shiloh,' Neal repeated as he took down the keywords on a purple writing pad. 'You know dear, you could just put this in to any search engine on any computer.'

'Of course I could, but then I would be at home in front of a laptop, and things don't happen on the web, they happen out here. Solving crime is a team sport.'

'You're just watching me sit in front of a laptop.'

'And you look wonderful doing it. I'd miss you if we didn't have these times together.'

'This,' Neal tapped his computer, 'is the library of the modern age. Much investigation is done at such machines. You should invest in a decent computer, Catherine.'

'But what for? I have you to help me work.'

'Well, if nothing else, what about pleasure?'

Catherine smiled her most satisfied smile, regaining some of her *joie de vivre* that had been missing since bumflowergate. 'My dear Neal, gin comes in bottles and I can use my hand in amusing ways. Why should I waste time with a modem?'

Neal smiled slowly, like a drunken pastor. 'Did you say something ribald dear? I swear I'm going deaf.'

'I didn't say a word.'

Catherine's mobile chirped Stravinsky.

'Boris.' She answered, then paused, 'Really? Did you follow?' She paced up and down as she listened to Boris. Neal continued his search, vaguely listening.

'No, a complete disaster would be if you stayed at that awful pub. Hmm, interesting. I think you can have the rest of the day off. Meet me for a constitutional at five? The Palace? Oh yes, you do work there, how lovely for you.'

Neal turned from his typing as he realised that Catherine was no longer talking with Boris but looking directly at him.

'Have you found any meanings for the fingers being severed?'

'They were referring to the proverbial cookie jar?'

Catherine did withering looks; she'd mastered the art at school. The one she gave Neal now could have killed a small swan. Luckily, Neal's good cheer could not be thwarted even by this. It was like trying to intimidate Buddha.

'There are a great deal of possibilities, Catherine. Why the urgency?'

'I had Boris trailing a man; he lost him, tried to find him by retracing his steps and found a card with a picture of a hand minus fingers, and a photo of himself.'

'That he hadn't taken?'

'The conversation we just had would have been different if he had.'

'Could it be a warning?' Neal asked, without taking his eyes off the screen.

'More likely a show-off. Watching the watcher is always impressive. I'm choosing to see it as we've got them rattled.'

Neal straightened in his chair and puffed out his chest a little.

'Indeed, we Indians have always felt that when someone has us in their sights and we haven't a clue who or where they are, we have them right where we want them. Must be why we win so many wars.'

'Oh please, you run the world and enjoy the most profitable cricket league on earth; I'll know who they are sooner or later.'

'When they're cutting your fingers off?'

'When they try.'

'This Asher fellow, did he seem Indian?' Neal asked.

'No. I'm not sure where his heritage lies, though I have the feeling it's fascinating.'

'The reason I ask is that an Asher was written about in the local paper three years ago. His name is Asher Light. I wondered if he were native American.'

'I was told his name was Marr,' Catherine replied. 'Is there a photo?'

Neal's fingers on the keyboard made the sound of tiny spots of mud hitting a tent roof and then he spun the screen around. 'That our hero?'

'Yes, that's him,' Catherine confirmed.

'Doesn't look native American, though I grant he's quite attractive.'

'You think so, Neal?'

'Cheekbones like that. Could be one of your exes.'

'Hush Neal, this is work.'

The story was about Asher showing local Steiner schoolchildren the basics of the new age world: crystals, meditation and sacred geometry. The photo was of him pushing a crystal in the close vision of some long haired seven-year-old boy who looked like he was about to explode in excitement. The story was dated three years earlier, and was in the local *Express* paper.

'That just confirms that he's a professional hippie. Anything connecting him to the victim?'

'Aside from the fact that they were a couple?' Neal raised his eyebrows and kept typing. 'Here you are, from the Jewel Real Estate feedback page archives: "Thanks to Cassandra Pierce for your help finding us our home. May peace be your future." It's from Asher, Shining Way.'

'So that's how they met,' Catherine said. 'A strange match, real estate and enlightenment.'

'Opposites attract.'

'I have her address; are you ready? Flat 12, 28 Mitchell Street, Brunswick East.'

Catherine repeated it to herself. 'Thanks, I'll have a look after this.'

'No break and enter, Catherine.'

'I'll not deviate from the path of righteousness, I'll just peek over a fence or two while I'm at it.'

'Hmm.'

As Neal clicked and typed, Catherine sat and went over the crime scene in her mind. The body faced northwards, encircled by the waves of her spilled blood. She stared in the clear light towards the sheaf. It seemed strange to Catherine that pagan rites would involve a corpse facing northward. Wouldn't towards the sun and the coming summer make more sense? The sheaf was at head height, Boris' rather than her own. Was it there prior, or was it a prop, left as a message or part of a rite post-mortem, the same way her fingers were cut?

After a few minutes Neal groaned. 'Oh, no, no, no,' he said, rubbing his forehead.

A terror gripped Catherine. Had she been scratching her buttocks?

Then Neal read: '*Having descended to Earth a man and walking among men for the first thirty-three years of his life, he has awoken as the glory and the mediator. The knower of all and the lover of Earth. He has healed and taught his wisdom in the quiet corners to the poor and the rich and whispered truths that he has remembered from his ancient lives. He has taken these teachings, these knowings, which have lain dormant since the dawn of time until his return and given them to humanity. His gift: The Way.*'

Catherine looked crestfallen. 'That's Asher? The messiah lives in Brunswick?'

'That's not him, that's daddy.'

'Who is?'

'Alexander Marr.'

'I assume that's a name, but I don't know it.'

'That's probably because...' Neal started reading again. '*Your soul has not yet reached the cosmic maturity to come into his presence and breathe his name.*'

'I see.' Catherine smiled. 'Yes I can barely cosmically touch my toes, let alone breathe a tosser's name.' She shook her head. 'Famous family.'

'He's a guru; he is our saviour, apparently,' Neal informed her, 'and you too can hear his initial teachings for just $16.95, or $14.90 for the download.'

'No thanks, I think my soul should remain cosmically immature for a while longer.'

'Would you like me to continue with the biography?'

'No, just make me up a highlights reel while you research the wheat and fingers thing. What I was hoping for was a motive, but such things don't come up with the first Google, do they?'

Neal rubbed his chin as he continued reading about Alexander Marr. 'Why would we need you if they did?'

'To make excellent hats, which is what I need to be doing right now.'

Catherine's phone beeped on the arm of her chair and vibrated a message. From Brittany, Catherine's favourite policewoman, accepting her invitation to discuss Parisian style and local intrigue in an hour.

'Catherine, I've just found this.' He spun the laptop theatrically and spilt his tea, swearing in Punjabi under his breath. Catherine looked at the article, dated almost three decades earlier, and saw a photo of a stern, moonfaced man getting into a police car. He scowled at the camera, his head framed by a receding shock of dark hair. His handcuffs were held close to his body length tunic. The article was short.

Spiritualist Alexander Marr was today arrested for allegedly assaulting a female disciple. Police attended his Carlton headquarters following claims that a 17-year old girl, who cannot be named, was harmed. She is believed to been studying at the movement's mansion.

The assault claims were made after the girl was found staggering on Lygon Street and told those who went to her aid that she had been abused during a ritual. The Canning Street property has been leased by Marr's movement – The Way – for 10 years. Marr was released on bail and is due to face court next month. The victim was taken to St Vincent's Hospital where she is in a stable condition.

Catherine looked back up at Neal. 'Can you look a bit further into our great guru? See if The Way is making any money?'

Neal made a face, he was a proud man who almost never did anything illegal and it pained him how often Catherine asked him to check Australian Tax Office records through cyber back channels. Catherine, of course, knew all the buttons to push.

'Think of the tales you will tell your grandchildren about the killers you brought to justice. Think of when you found the storage space in that kidnapping case. We never would have found those kids without you. Remember how impressed June was?'

Neal blushed a little. 'I suppose it's for the greater good.'

Catherine squeezed his shoulder. 'Our cause is true and righteous.'

'That's what everyone says. It's what history will record that worries me.'

'Thanks Neal. May your soul grow a cosmic beard.'

Once outside, she set out for Mitchell Street. While she walked, Catherine mused on the facts, the rumours and the unknown knowns. She was certain that Melissa would not kill anyone. Eccentricities aside.

Of course there was no proof of this yet, so she could understand Williams' interest: weapon, proximity, a motive – however flimsy. But even when she tried, she just did not believe that her friend could have killed Cassandra.

She would need to speak with Asher again to learn more about Cassandra. She would need to get past Shiloh. She thought of the article about Asher written three years ago that Neal had found; there was no mention of Shiloh. Catherine wondered if he was in the family business. Although, if Shiloh also worked at a place called The Shining Way, he was unlikely to be a dry-cleaner.

Would a professional guru kill his lover? Catherine knew that anyone could kill their lover. Strong emotion was what drove people to kill. A loving hand could become a fist given the right circumstances.

It seemed that Asher's father had had brushes with the law regarding women.

Then there was Marcus Frawley, who was worried about something and obviously had little love for Cassandra. Boris had said Frawley was frightened of the long-haired man. Whoever he was.

A rousing of the itch on her behind brought her thoughts to Alice the witch; surely she needed to be questioned. That left Cassandra's family, friends, rivals in real estate, and local residents of East Brunswick high on Catherine's list of people to watch. Also, she needed to speak with whomever Cassandra had been drinking with on the night of her death. At some point, too, she would need to make some hats. She checked her watch: 12.30, not enough hours, too much to do.

Catherine came to the place that Cassandra Pierce used to call home. It was a sturdy red brick block on the corner of a small side street. Across the road was a park where a grandmother pushed a toddler on a swing. The child squealed with delight, distracting Catherine so much that she barely noticed the people in the grey Holden parked fifty metres up the road until it was almost too late.

She aborted her original mission and kept walking, past the two bored men in the car. Thirties, clean cut, grey suits. Homicide police. Catherine trying to break into Cassandra's house, after being present when police found her body, would be enough to have her locked up for a few hours at least. Good to know the police were keeping an open enough mind to be watching the victim's house. Answers would, for now, have to come from somewhere else. The itch on her backside told her exactly where to begin.

Catherine turned for Stewart Street and the halfway house that Melissa had talked about. Stewart Lodge was an eighty-bed facility run by the Department of Human Services. Catherine had known about it for years and often spoke to residents as she passed by. It was a pale brick building, surrounded by a short fence made of the same material. Today an obese man in a yellow T-shirt sat on the fence. As she approached, he smiled at her and waved. Catherine waved back, murmuring a hello as she moved up the driveway to where she assumed the office would be.

The office was a cramped room, dominated by posters advocating respect and acceptance. A red-bearded man in his thirties wearing an un-ironed blue shirt was sitting behind a desk piled with folders and paper. He looked up and smiled. 'Hi.'

'Hi, I'm Catherine Kint. I'm looking for someone who I think lives here.'

'Sure. Name?'

'Alice.'

'Alice who?'

'I'm not sure. She has dark hair, about forty-five and has a nose.'

The man touched his own, as if making sure he hadn't gone to a separate dimension where having a nose was noteworthy. Catherine corrected herself; she must be getting hungry.

'Sorry, I mean to say she has a distinct nose.'

'OK. Why are you looking for this person?' He was still smiling, but it was professional.

'It's a personal matter.'

'I'm afraid without any other explanation I can't give out any information, even to confirm if an Alice with a nose lives here.' He tilted his head a little. 'Sorry.'

Catherine moved closer to his desk. 'I know this is odd, but it's vital I speak with Alice. I'm hoping she can help me with a medical problem.'

His face hardened. 'I'm sorry, many of our residents are recovering from addiction. Please get your medical help elsewhere. I wish you the best of luck.'

'Oh no, that's not what I meant.' Catherine smiled her most sober and normal smile. 'Did you hear about the woman who died just past Lygon Street yesterday?'

He nodded.

'I'm afraid it's to do with that. You see...'

He held up a hand, the smile had gone. 'Ms Kint, the residents here are under the duty of care of the department. If you're police, then contact our police liaison. If you're not police, I can't imagine why you would want to speak with a resident about a violent crime.'

Catherine raised both hands with open palms. 'No, it's just that she may be in some danger.'

'Ms Kint, my job is in part ensuring that the residents are not harassed. If there is an Alice staying here then I assure you that she will be protected. I don't think we have anything further to discuss.'

He wasn't angry, or even annoyed, but his tone brooked no argument.

'No, clearly not.' Catherine left him to his snowdrift of paperwork. As she walked out, she tried to remember the last time a conversation had gone that badly sober.

Out the front, the obese man in yellow was still enjoying the fresh air. He again waved to Catherine, smiling through broken teeth.

'Hello.'

'Hello, do you live here?'

'I do,' he said. 'I'm Tom,' and held out his hand. Catherine's own was dwarfed in his grip.

'I'm Catherine. Do you know Alice who lives here?'

'Oh yeah, everyone knows Big Nose.' He laughed and almost fell off his perch on the brick fence.

'Have you seen her today?'

He explored a nostril with his forefinger thoughtfully. 'Not today. She was here yesterday. Not before. Hey.'

'Yes?'

'Would you like to be my girlfriend?' He smiled beautifully, despite the damaged chompers. It was one of the most sincere smiles Catherine had ever seen.

'Not today, Tom. Let's just be friends, today. Will you tell me if you see Alice?'

'Sure. Bye, friend.'

There was a lesson, Catherine thought as she walked away. Don't go to the official if the street has the information. The residents at Stewart Lodge would be a mixed bag, of course they would. The question was if anyone there would be capable of planning the murder of Cassandra after putting in place the red herrings, such as the doll, weeks earlier.

It seemed unlikely, leaving Catherine feeling no closer to any kind of progress. It was time to find more information.

At times like these you need a special someone. Like a police officer who loves hats.

'You're not serious?' Britt sounded incredulous. A tall woman, she made an exaggerated pout in the mirror, pushing the hat to the top of her head, her arm collecting straight blonde hair as she did so.

'I am, Britt. She's a client, she's a friend, and she is innocent.' Catherine's kettle iron belched small punctuations of steam to emphasise the conviction in her voice. The hot mist obscured her face momentarily. Had you never seen a milliner work before, you may have thought of a magician disappearing in a puff of smoke.

'Bloody unlucky if she's innocent.'

Around each wall in the small room, which was situated in the shopfront below Catherine's apartment, were a dozen hats in various forms of completion. Behind Catherine's workstation were accessories laid out fastidiously that included feathers, netting, glues, Petersham ribbons and a meticulously selected array of fabrics. Up high on top of the long cupboards along the east wall were three of Catherine's four blocks – bucket, brim and dome, with a small stepladder for easy access. Looking down on proceedings was a framed photograph of Audrey Hepburn smiling enticingly in Holly Golightly's wide brim.

Senior Constable Brittany Houden could have been a model. People often say that of a beautiful woman, but in her case it was true. There were other officers who worked the beat out of Broadmeadows Police Station who would be described as attractive women, some even beautiful, but Britt was that other-worldly kind of stunning. She was offered a four-year catwalk contract at age seventeen. She had turned it down due to a strong sense of civic duty and because she found most people in the fashion world to be vapid, obtuse and incredibly annoying. When she had heard that Catherine was leaving crime scene investigation to become a milliner, she made a point of telling Catherine exactly that. This act of honesty cemented her as one of Catherine's close friends, and she had been given leave to model in one of Catherine's first millinery shows.

Years later they had a mutually beneficial, if secret, relationship. Catherine was a milliner who sometimes solved crimes, Brittany was a fast-rising policewoman who could not resist the delights of a fine hat.

They traded confidences for the joint goals of finding the truth and looking fabulous. Today, Britt was checking all the angles of a duck-egg blue pillbox that Catherine had just finished and discussing the inner rumblings of the police case against Melissa.

'I had no idea of names, of course, but I had heard the evidence is a snap. Your friend has the knife, motive, recorded intent and vicinity. The victim was found a hundred metres from her back fence. The only reason they haven't charged her yet is because they want to check the boyfriend's alibi,' Britt told Catherine.

'The knife aside, the evidence is mostly circumstantial, plus I recall vividly there being two knives, one of which is not with Melissa.' Catherine was speaking from within a steaming cloud as she worked on her bowler block. The iron expelled more steam as her hand moulded the aqua felt into the desired shape.

Britt waved away steam to eyeball her friend. 'Tell me, if you weren't her friend and you were working the case, what would you think?'

Catherine was quiet for a few seconds, then scowled. 'I agree it looks bad, but I don't think Mel would kill. She's also told me she didn't know anything about Cassandra and hasn't kept tabs since the VCAT thing.'

'What about the doll?'

'Point in Mel's favour. If you're going to gruesomely kill someone, why would you then put a doll with the same markings outside your door for all to see?'

'But there's a problem there. Occasionally people do want to get caught,' Britt said.

'You think Mel is one of those stupidly chosen few?'

'I'm not on the case. The fact that she's close to you makes me doubt that she's stupid. The general feeling of the cops, off the record, is that she's a fame-addicted whacko.'

From beneath her steaming cloud, Catherine tilted the kettle away from the felt and closed her eyes. Quietly, she said, 'She wasn't always so attracted to the spotlight, I assure you.' Then louder: 'That looks good on you.'

'Would you have something in red?' Britt asked. 'I've just got this great new dress for the races.'

'Have a look at the felts over by the window. Now tell me about other suspects. What was the boyfriend up to?'

'Classified.'

'And that hat will be $1500 then, cash or credit card?'

'We're making enquiries.'

'Not good enough. Haven't we done this dance enough times? Has it ever gone badly? If you didn't help me, those girls from last year would still be missing.'

'The end doesn't always justify the means.'

'I'm not asking you to torture. Just tell me about other suspects. Starting with Asher Marr.'

Britt was silent as she stared at the hat. Then she spoke. 'He was with his brother all night at home. The shop assistant locked up about seven and they were already in for the night.'

'Brothers are good for that kind of alibi, aren't they? You have no suspicion?'

'Of course. He was interviewed for about five hours today. Nothing. Just a grieving boyfriend.'

'What about family?' Catherine asked.

'There are routine checks being done on hers, though there are no criminal records. Also known contacts in real estate, anyone who has repeatedly left messages for her at work. This is the colour.' Britt held up a Persian red.

'You want that in a pillbox? Show me a photo of the dress.'

Brittany passed her phone to Catherine through the steam. Catherine looked at the photo and flexed her neck thoughtfully.

'You sure you wouldn't want to go the other way and use a brim? They never go out of fashion.'

'No, I'm going through a Jackie Onassis thing.'

'No problem, I'll have it for you next week.'

'If you're trying to solve the crime, you'll have your hands full. Make it a fortnight and call it even.'

Britt left through the back door, leaving Catherine to work with the bowler block and concentrate on her many thoughts. The world was a small place. Williams being on the case was proof of that, but it seemed beyond the pale that the killer would place a piece of evidence as intriguing as a doll at Melissa's house two weeks prior to the crime. Assuming the doll and the crime were connected, and she would bet three fingers they were, Mel was being set up. That made two victims she was working for.

The phone rang. Catherine looked up at the red clock in the corner as she put the iron down. It had only been 45 minutes since Britt had left, but long enough for time to stop as it did when Catherine worked on hats.

'Neal, you're pulling me away from paid work!'

'And you're pulling me from teaching children their tonal intervals, which is also paid work. Let's not forget whose idea this was.'

Catherine leaned back in her chair. She rested the kettle against its stand and stared out through the steam, out the window, and on to Albion Street. 'What have you found about the brothers Marr?'

'Nothing of note. Catherine, I hope you are sitting down.'

'I am.'

'I was doing some background in the courts data and…' Neal sounded uncharacteristically unsure. 'I found something…that might interest you.'

'To do with the case?'

'Yes.'

'Neal, it's unlike you to be hesitant with me. What is it? Are Asher and Shiloh in some kind of trouble?'

'Not so much them. It's Melissa.'

Catherine's grip on the phone tightened.

'At least, it could be her.'

'Tell me.' The kettle was cooling rapidly beside her.

For the next eight minutes Catherine sat almost completely still. At one point she swore softly.

When the phone call ended, Catherine left the studio. It was all she could do not to slam the door.

The kettle was almost cold.

6

Nothing evolves on a clean surface.
~ Boris Shakhovskoy

Melissa's hair was wrapped in a blue towel when she opened the door. 'What's up?'

Catherine walked past her into the dark hallway. Her hands did not move from hip level. Melissa scurried behind her, after she closed the door.

'Knocking like that I thought you must have been the cops. What is it? Catherine why are you so…?'

Catherine reached the kitchen and spun around, facing her friend.

'Tell me who Melissa Denise Dalton is.' Her voice was low with rage.

Mel's face turned to stone. Then her bottom lip started trembling.

Catherine continued: 'Did you go to jail for grievous bodily harm fifteen years ago?'

As Catherine watched her friend, the part of her that wasn't furious noticed how frightened Melissa looked. Mel's mouth barely moved as she said, 'Yes.'

Catherine walked three steps to Melissa's large black table, placed both palms down on it and was silent.

Melissa whispered from across the room, 'I should have told you.'

'That's another bloody understatement,' Catherine said, fiercely. 'There's enough crap flying around without more of it coming from you.' She turned again, this time slowly.

Melissa looked like she was melting. 'How did you find out?'

'The same way they will. Bloody hell, Mel! You're not a possible suspect anymore, you're an ex-crim with proven form.' As Catherine spoke she gesticulated at the blank spot on the wall where a shield with two knives had hung for years, now sitting in the evidence storage room at St Kilda Road police station.

'It hasn't been the best day. I'm sorry, Catherine.'

'Is there anything else I should know? One more revelation like this and I'll walk.'

A steely look came into Mel's eye. 'How could you say that?'

Catherine could more than match it. 'You'd be amazed what I could say right now, but maybe you wouldn't, because I've always told you the truth about me.'

Most things in life ran off her like Chinese tea on duck fat. But being conned by a friend, even one who was trying to con everybody, was not something she could tolerate. Mel had the good sense to look cowed. Catherine continued: 'Now, if I wanted to talk to a witch about the rites stuff, who should I see?'

Mel looked hurt. 'Me.'

'You've gone from friend to unknown quantity. I need to be sure you didn't have anything to do with this.'

'Catherine, I swear—'

'Don't. I'm going to find out who killed Cassandra and I need to know I'm getting the right information. Right now, I don't know what to believe about you, Ms Dalton.'

Mel's tone was measured. 'Go to the bank next to the Penny Black Hotel. Ask for Kirsten. She'll help.'

Catherine nodded, tempering the steel in her voice: 'Attagirl, you're learning. What happened with the grievous bodily harm?'

'Short version: I was in a share house with three other girls. One of them, Angela, starts going out with this footy player named Travis. Big guy, strong. He's nice enough. Then he drinks and a different guy comes out. Petty. Possessive. Angela and I had been close, but that changed when she fell in love with him. I was cool with that. Love conquers all, and such.

'After three months the magic starts to fade and she begins to see he has a dark side. She starts talking with me again, hoping he'll back off. He doesn't, the jealousy kicks in and he starts getting violent. He's a big guy and after I see the bruises I get really pissed off. He came round one night, started pushing me in the kitchen. I took out a knife and stabbed him. Just in the stomach; and a bit in the arm.'

She looked at the ceiling. 'It went to trial. I did three months, came out, did an anger management course, and took my mother's maiden name to make a clean break.'

Catherine let the story waft in the air for a minute. 'Any other surprises?'

'That's it. Aside from parking tickets, I've never been in trouble with the law.'

Catherine idly scratched her ear. 'So what happened to Angela?'

'Travis came out of hospital, joined AA and hasn't had a drink since. Angela married him. He wrote to me a few years ago and thanked me for the wake-up call.'

Catherine breathed out slowly, the anger subsiding. The whole thing was so like Mel: the good intentions, the bad judgment and the positive contribution to a bad situation. 'And thus let no good deed go unpunished.'

Catherine sat down at the table and Melissa put the kettle on. They sat with their own thoughts while it boiled. Melissa slowly dried her hair. Catherine felt her stomach uncoil. She rarely got angry and now was enjoying the after-effects. A thought struck her. 'By the way, how old are you?'

'Thirty-nine.' Melissa gave a little smile.

'Right, anything else?'

Melissa passed Catherine a peppermint tea that she had conjured up. Her voice was quiet but steady. 'I've never hurt anyone physically since then. It was when I was in prison that I could see what a life wasted was. Please Catherine, I need you. If you can't find who killed this girl, and police find out about Travis, then I'm done for a long time.'

'I won't let that happen.' Catherine put down the mug. 'But now I have my date with the police.'

An hour later, Catherine was in a police interview room, a small room without natural light. On the table in front of her was an instant coffee, Ben, her lawyer, was beside her and opposite her was Detective Williams. Beside him sat Watkins, a fellow detective Catherine recognised as Williams' driver from the day before. He had a stern expression between two wing-nut ears.

'Ms Kint, would you mind discussing the events in the twenty-four hours leading up to you finding the body of Cassandra Pierce between eight-thirty and nine-thirty on the morning of the twenty-first of September?'

'Really, from eight-thirty on the twentieth?'

'Everything's relevant, Ms Kint.' Williams' eyes shifted from the dossier in his hand to give her a hard look.

Catherine inhaled deeply and focused on Watkins' left ear.

'I woke up on the twentieth at around 8am at my home. I made coffee, ate fruit toast and considered which hats to work on. As I'm sure you know milliners are very busy at this time of year leading up to the spring racing carnival. I also had a series of brims that a favourite client had ordered for her wedding in October. I took the risk of blocking two of them in a session and that took up the next ninety-five minutes, taking us to 11.38am. I took a break and read the morning papers on my balcony. Is this boring you?'

Williams' smile juxtaposed with his glazed eyes. 'You could have said you made hats all morning.'

'I did that all afternoon too, will that do?'

'I think you might give us a bit more detail if we go slowly.'

'By 1pm I had eaten a light lunch and realised I was out of a certain colour of ribbon. I took my Vespa to a haberdashery supply shop in Coburg and returned to my apartment. I spoke on the phone to my client for fifteen minutes – she was in a state because it turns out that her bridesmaid has gone to Richard Nylon for advice and wanted to make the hats more flamboyant. Thankfully, there was still time and I was able to sort it out. I worked on them until 4.58pm when I ceased working for the day.

'I spent the evening at the respectable tavern known as the Glasgow Palace where I stayed until roughly 3am. At which point I returned home and slept. The following morning I walked to Lygon Street, East Brunswick, where I breakfasted. It was during this meal that I was phoned by Boris Shakhovskoy. I met him in the alley in which the body was found. Soon after, we were joined by the police.'

'Boris Shakhovskoy is a barman at the Glasgow Palace?'

'Yes.'

'Was he involved in your unofficial investigation of the kidnapping last year?'

'Yes, Boris was with me when we found the girls.'

Williams' mouth pursed and he made a show of jotting something on a notepad. 'And did you speak with him the night of the twentieth of September?'

'I did.'

'What did you discuss?'

'Whether half the books now considered classics would have been in that category if they hadn't broken the conventional rules of their time. Whether *The Master and Margarita* would be looked upon so fondly if it had been written in another country either fifty years before, or after, it was written. And, if any piece of art was truly detached from the cultural environment in which it was created.'

Williams looked at Catherine. 'Great.'

Catherine smiled wanly.

Williams continued: 'Did you organise to meet with Mr Shakhovskoy the next day?'

'No.'

'Did Mr Shakhovskoy know where you would be?'

'Yes, he does occasionally join me for breakfast.'

'So he knew that you would be close at hand on the day?'

'Yes.'

Williams leaned close to her; Catherine could count the broken capillaries on his cheek.

'Why do you think he rang you,? Why not just call us?'

'He did.'

'And then he called you. Why?'

Catherine stared coolly: 'Because I would know what to do.'

'You would know what to do,' Williams repeated. His face darkened. 'Did you have contact with Melissa Zamansky that day?'

'I had a voicemail from her after I returned home.'

'You didn't speak to her prior to leaving the crime scene.'

'No.'

'Did you send an email?'

'No.'

'A text?'

'No.'

'Prior to yesterday, when was the last time you had contact with Melissa Dalton?'

Catherine's gut twisted. He knew.

'I believe that she goes by the name Zamansky these days.'

'Catherine, I think you didn't know about her past.' Williams' look was paternal.

Ben put a hand down on the table and leaned in, 'I don't know where this is going.'

'It's OK, Ben, I know where it's going.' Catherine hadn't broken eye contact with Williams who continued, softly.

'I think friends can disappoint. I think you were probably disappointed today.' He paused. 'When you found out she had stabbed a man in the past. You were seen going to her house, angry. I suspect you found out what we did today. I knew as soon as I mentioned the name Dalton.'

'Yes, of course, I was disappointed.'

Williams leaned closer over the table. 'But you still believe she's innocent? Have you seen the article linking Ms Zamansky to the victim published last year?'

'Yes.'

'Compelling reading, given the circumstances wouldn't you say?'

'People make mistakes. She didn't kill Cassandra.'

'People make mistakes,' he repeated, as if weighing the concept. 'Yes they do,' Williams said quietly. 'Just know, Catherine, if you know someone who has made a mistake – even a big one – you tell them to talk to me about it.'

Boris' mood was pensive when they met. He stared into his pint and kept half smiling as if trying to dislodge a piece of bread from his left cheek.

Catherine put up with this for thirty-eight minutes before she cracked. 'I can't see why you're letting it upset you.'

'I feel beaten.'

'You were. You were spying, they spied better. Now drink up and cheer up.'

'I just thought I'd notice someone watching me,' he said.

'Yes, I know someone paying attention to you should stick out like a sore thumb, but why worry?' She counted blessings on her fingers. 'No one got killed that wasn't already dead; you obviously rattled them, and if stalking someone as a paid private investigator only to be stalked back isn't your cup of tea, you can go work for the public service.'

That did the trick; it always did. Boris straightened up. 'I don't want to work for the public service.'

'That's the spirit!' Catherine's hands waved like she was a gospel singer.

'I want an interesting life.'

'It'll have its moments.'

'I want to die young and leave a beautiful corpse.' Boris slapped the bar.

'One out of two's not a disaster!'

'Leon, let's have some scotch!'

His boss poured the liquor. Boris had a tab running, which ate into his wages each week. Had he not found further employment he would find it difficult to save and would likely never see a test match in Jamaica. As it was, it would take about thirty years to get there. Boris thought of the sun and the cricket as he sipped his drink in quiet satisfaction. Bad mood banished, he scanned the room.

'You know, my eyes aren't what they once were but I think that bloke is looking at you.'

Catherine's brown eyes saw, on the far side of the bar, a handsome stranger whom she'd met only recently. Asher Marr was quietly watching her. Catherine slid from her stool as she smiled at him. 'Boris, I think I may have to do some solo work tonight.'

Boris nodded thoughtfully. 'He's prettier than Frawley.'

'No one ever called the universe fair, Boris.'

Asher was moving towards her with a drink in his hand. How long he had been watching, she didn't know. He looked strained and a little tired, but Catherine – forever looking to celebrate the world she lived in – revelled in just how pretty he was. High cheekbones and proud features framed by wavy and seemingly edible hair. He had a face that could pull off a beret as easily as a bowler; it would be a pleasure to watch his face transformed by the perfect hat. Catherine was taken by his dancer-like movements. His natural grace could get him barred from an establishment like this. This was a two left-foot pub, all thinkers, no dancers.

'Hello, Catherine.' He held a hand out. She liked that he didn't bother introducing himself.

'Hi, Asher.'

'I wanted to find you. I heard this was the place,' he said with a small smile. 'There are worse places to run a business.'

'Well done on finding me, but this is pleasure.'

He put his drink on the bar. 'I need your business. I'm under suspicion, and I think they're following me.'

'Police?'

'Have to be.'

'Why come to me?'

'I found out what you do. I have some smart friends and you have a reputation. I thought while you're around in my life you might want to find out what happened so I can stop looking over my shoulder.'

'You make it sound so appealing. Anything else?'

He sipped his drink. Saw hers was dry, gestured to Leon while he kept speaking. 'Cassandra's dead, I'm being interviewed, the police are wasting their time and I need to know what happened.'

'Sounds like we want the same thing.'

'Yes, but one of us *needs* it.' He passed her the drink, pointedly.

The glass stopped momentarily, then resumed its trajectory to her mouth. She drank slowly and deliberately. 'Don't tell me what I need.'

'I meant me.' He looked away. 'I don't care how much gin you like. I just need to know who did it and why.' Only his mouth moved when he spoke, the rest of him was almost tight.

It occurred to Catherine that he was angry, but controlling it.

'Any thoughts?'

'Wasn't me.' He stared at her.

'Wasn't me either, Asher. Then again I'm not a suspect. Don't look at me like that.'

His face softened and he looked away.

'Damn. I didn't mean to look at you any way. Everyone at home is being so nice and the police are going over and over...' his hand made a circle motion while he finished his drink. He ran a hand over his face wearily. 'Sorry about my brother. He's on edge.'

'Don't apologise. I was knocking on a door that said closed after your lover was murdered.'

'But since then I found out that you solved a kidnapping case last year, resulting in two young girls being returned to their families.'

'How did you know about the kidnappings? The family kept me out of the papers.'

'I know some people.' He smiled and Catherine thought it was one of the most pleasant things she had seen all day. 'I asked some people about you,' he continued, 'about this elegant woman who came to the door asking questions. They told me about the kidnapping and a few other exploits, and said if I wanted to talk to you I should come here.'

'Who exactly did you speak to?'

'I can't name my sources, but they're fans of yours.'

'So not the police then?'

'They haven't mentioned you and I've spent the past two days with them. When I wasn't at the morgue.'

'I'm sorry.'

He looked sad. 'It's so often the boyfriend, police say.' He gestured again to Leon, this time for himself, checked her drink and ordered one for her, without asking. The gin was sailing down.

'How are you holding up?' she asked kindly.

'Not your concern.' It was just a statement, but it threw Catherine. Asher appeared not to notice and continued. 'I just want to know,' he said tapping the bar, looking to Leon to pay.

'I can't promise, but I have my own interests in finding out as well,' Catherine said, as she ushered him into a seat.

'So I heard. You're friends with that witch,' Asher's voice dropped as he said it, a hint of contempt.

'Her name's Melissa.'

'I know it is, but until I know she didn't do it I can't quite say her name.'

'I'm talking to you, and you're a suspect, too.'

He looked at her hard. 'Innocent until proven guilty, even the cops have to go by that.'

'I'm not a cop.'

'I hear you couldn't hack it.'

She eyes narrowed. 'If you'd feel more comfortable talking to the police…'

'No. Sorry.' His hand fell quickly on hers. 'I know you'll find out.'

He was still holding her hand; his eyes locked on hers, grief and need pouring off him.

'Do you believe in the spiritual, Catherine?'

She extricated her hand. 'Not at first sight, no. Tell me about the last time you saw her.'

'Two nights ago, at her place. She was about to go to the bar.'

'Which bar?'

'Atticus Finch. She was meeting with a Sydney real estate guy. I wasn't entirely sure. We had a fight.'

'Did you fight about her moving to Sydney?'

He paused. 'No.'

'What about?'

'Just couple stuff.'

'It could be important.' She watched him think, weighing up the right words or the white lies.

'Other girls.'

'Ah.' She took a drink, cooling herself. She could hardly blame the other girls.

'It's not… I didn't…' He faltered, his hand on hers again. She looked at it. His eyes widened in apology and he moved his chair back.

'I wasn't cheating on her. We were just having a few issues. Catherine, I'm sorry, could we do this another time?' His face had started to sag.

'One last question: who would want to kill her?'

'Did you ever meet her?'

'No.'

'She was quiet and loving and smart, but she liked to win.'

'That can make things hard.'

He took a moment. 'We were together for over three years. Enough time to really know someone. I think in a lifetime you really only get to know a few people. She was one, and it was worth it.'

Catherine, without thinking, looked across to Boris. Asher followed the look. Boris was laughing and hiccupping at the same time. Leon was reaching across the bar and slapping him on the back. 'Your man?'

Catherine shook her head. 'Just someone I really know. So Cassandra liked to win. Do you think that had something to do with what happened to her?'

He finished his drink. 'Not now. I'm sorry.'

'Asher, who could have done this?'

'I don't know how many people would like to kill her. But a lot wanted her to lose.'

His face was hardening again. Catherine pushed on.

'Anyone in particular?'

'No. I have no idea.' He began walking away.

'You say you want my help. Stay, I need to talk to you.'

Catherine followed him outside. As the door closed behind them,

Catherine caught his shoulder, he stopped, but didn't turn around. He slowly rubbed his face with both hands. Catherine saw his eyes wet with tears and put an arm around him. His body was as taut as rope; she almost forgot the case and her decorum to offer him sympathy at home. After a minute, he regained his composure. He stood straight in the night and looked towards the sky. His eyes were beautiful and wet. Catherine felt if she touched him she wouldn't stop, so she left him alone. He looked at her.

'I know you don't do spirituality on first dates, but I asked for you. Just before you came.'

His hand was briefly on her face and then he was gone, leaving Catherine feeling like she had just stepped off a spaceship.

7

If you want faith don't seek knowledge.
~ Alexander Marr

awn was still many hours off, and all of the northern suburbs were mostly turning in their sleep. Boris and Catherine slowly walked to her apartment down Albion Street. Boris was drinking from his knock-off stubby and Catherine was still mulling over her discussion with Asher.

'It didn't seem right.'

'Which bit?' Boris asked, wiping foam from his lips with the back of his hand. 'The part where he wanted to talk to you, or the part where you just wanted to sleep with him?'

'I would usually welcome the distraction of lust getting in the way of professionalism.' Catherine kicked a stone. 'Sadly, I'm not making him an array of hats. It's important that I'm focused. Yet there he was, all charm and grief mixed up. Messing with my chi.'

'His girlfriend was killed just days ago, he has that aura of "I'm so alive by proxy" thing going. Like Spock in *Star Trek 3*.' Boris took a pull of his beer. 'Do you think he has something to do with it?'

'The police don't think so. I checked with Britt, and she confirmed he spent a good deal of time with police, his brother too. Their stories corroborate. He seemed very keen for me to find out the truth.' Another stone became an impromptu soccer ball for Catherine's nimble toes.

'He's very clever, though. A bit disconcerting, too. I'm not sure he wasn't doing the same thing to me that I was doing to him.'

'What's that exactly?' Boris worked through the double negative.

'You know dear, just trying to find out what goes on underneath the surface of a face, trying to see what's not being said, feeling out preferences, trying to work out if they're holding a candle or a gun.'

'Uh, huh. And him trying to read you is terrible because?'

'He should be grieving. Should be in shock. He seems a bit erratic, but he was still very good at throwing me off guard. It's rude.'

'But you doing it is…?'

'Part of my job to find out who killed Cassandra and to make sure that Melissa doesn't end up framed for it.' She turned and faced him. 'My cause is noble, Boris. I thought you shared it.'

'Oh boots and all, Catherine,' he said disinterestedly. 'Should I do it, too?'

'What?'

'Feel out preferences for candles and guns?'

'Oh that.' Yet another stone found its way to the railway with a satisfying clang. Catherine was sure she could have been one of the soccering greats. 'In the same way that skateboards should levitate: it would be great if you could.'

'You're wonderful for my self-esteem.'

'Dear Boris, you've never had an ulterior motive in your life.' She put a hand on his shoulder. 'Take heart, the only reason you can't do that is because it doesn't occur to you.'

Boris sneered benignly. 'You make it sound like I've never seen Paris.'

'It's charming and noble.'

'I heard it was over-rated and expensive.'

'See, even when I'm nice you deflect. You don't need my praise.'

He shrugged. 'True, that's why I grew a beard. It's all I need.'

They walked down the quiet street, Boris pulling on his beer and Catherine practising her soccer moves. There were no sounds of trains, or birds, or industry, just a faint hum of the nearby power lines that reverberated across the narrow street. It was a nice moment. Then came the panicked screeching of tyres.

The car was a dark Audi or some similar make. Large and sleek, it came directly for them, engine roaring as it hurtled towards the footpath. The driver wore dark glasses and his hooded form was hunched over the steering wheel. Boris was suddenly in front of Catherine. His bulk obscured her view of the car within a couple of metres. Then it changed course, straightened to the road and pulled in close for the briefest of moments, tyres screeching. It went from what must have been 80 kilometres per hour to crawling in seconds. Boris stepped backwards into Catherine, his arms akimbo. Over Boris' shoulder Catherine saw the driver move. The streetlights flashed in his glasses. His arm rose over the driver window. Boris spun, clamped his arms about her and pushed her down. She saw a flash and felt warmth as an explosion hit the wall behind her. The sound in her ears was Boris grunting, glass breaking and the wumph of igniting flame.

There was a smell of sulphur as the car squealed off. Catherine rolled out from under Boris and tried to see the number plate. XRZ she read, but the numbers escaped her. She turned to Boris, he was grinning from the adrenaline. He wasn't bleeding anywhere obvious. Always good news.

'You all right?' Catherine noticed the blast had damaged her hearing; everything was muted.

'Always hated flash cars.' Boris' eyes were wide and he was breathing deeply.

'Your car's up the road. Let's go.' Catherine started running; the Audi could only be a few hundred metres away. She slowed as she realised Boris hadn't moved. Her hand flew to her head, exasperated. 'Boris?'

He stood peering at his grazed elbow and spoke without looking up. 'The car's gone, we can't catch up and you're too drunk to drive.'

'Oh come on!' Catherine wanted to give Boris a kick to the groin, but restrained herself; a girl is nothing without restraint.

'He's gone, Catherine, let's try and find out what the explosion was.'

Walking back, Boris found his beer, miraculously intact, and drained it. Catherine felt the adrenaline recede and looked at Boris, checking for anxiety. Boris was always better at this kind of thing when he wasn't alone. If there was someone to protect, he would just be brave without thinking about it. The projectile had missed them by centimetres and smashed into the brick wall of a warehouse. The street lamps were bright enough to see clear bottle glass stained black and scattered on the ground. The sulphurous smell still lingered and smelt oddly familiar.

Boris picked up pieces of glass as though the attacker may have left his name and contact details. Catherine was about to admonish him when he spoke. 'Sprite.'

He held up the shard, about the size of a guitar plectrum, with the tell-tale swirl of the 'ri' from the logo.

'Oh, that's just cheap,' Catherine began, 'if you're going to throw something flammable at me at least make it top shelf. Did he come straight from a nine-year-old's birthday party?'

'Not at this time of night, unless you know some night owl nine-year-olds.'

Catherine frowned. 'Birthday party…' She smelt the air.

Boris stood up. 'What?'

'Sparklers, children's sparklers, that's what this smells of. A simple missile made of a Sprite bottle and children's sparklers. No criminal master mind at work here.'

'I thought it could have been a hit man when I saw the big black car.'

Catherine snorted and looked at the sprite shard. 'Might have taken us out with a cap gun. We could have caught him Boris; I hate it when you do that.'

'I know how much you love a good car chase Catherine, but after all the day's excitement I just want to go home. Maybe you could get out Mario Kart or something?'

Catherine looked at him the way some people look at modern art.

She had decided not to wake Boris in the early morning. Some jobs needed a woman's touch and he was grumpy if he didn't get enough beauty sleep. As she made a coffee she watched him sleeping on her couch, Minty asleep on his chest. She left them there and rode her Vespa just a kilometre south. She could have walked, but she needed speed that morning. It was cool at seven; four hours before Cassandra's funeral. Catherine had chosen the full visor helmet, and in her bag she had a garishly large grey tweed cap, perfect for surveillance and concealing the effect of the helmet on her hairstyle.

She was, by her reckoning, about 218 metres from the doorway of The Shining Way: A Guided Life, less pretentiously known as the house of Asher and Shiloh Marr. She sat on a bench at Jewell train station, on the Upfield-bound side. She kept her eyes on the front of the shop and also the windows. She saw a curtain move once, briefly seeing Asher's face look towards the sky. If Catherine were discovered it would be embarrassing but not diabolical. She could always play the "falling for you" line. Or pretend she had an appointment in Fawkner.

Except it wasn't Asher she was interested in. Hours after having an explosive bottle thrown at her, Catherine was watching the man who had shown the most hostility towards her in the past forty-eight hours. She wanted to see what Shiloh Marr did with his time.

Across the tracks a phalanx of suit-wearing workers stood on the black platform waiting for city-bound trains. They rolled in every fifteen minutes as the peak hour began in earnest. As one rumbled past, she almost missed Shiloh as he walked on to the street. He was wearing dark track pants and runners, and looked around him before he tore off north. Catherine had enough time to swap her cap for the helmet and mount the Vespa.

This was where she assumed the going would become more difficult. Shiloh began running up a shared pathway for bikes and pedestrians. Her Vespa was not legal on this path, nor would it be conducive to remaining unseen. Still, Catherine had experience and let her instincts take over. Shiloh was going against the traffic and so Catherine took the blocks to Victoria Street where the running path crossed a road. She parked thirty metres from the intersection, counted to twenty in French and he appeared, turning west towards the park.

Catherine pretended to be adjusting her headlight as he passed on the other side of the road, but if he noticed he gave no sign. Catherine watched him in her rear-view mirror until he only appeared as a speck crossing to the soccer ovals a kilometre down the road. She U-turned and moved past the grounds, watching through her helmet visor as he moved to Gilpin Park. She swung up Pearson Street to the park's westernmost point, where she could see him moving in between the trees and tracks. Hidden by a large peppercorn tree she watched him as he came within 100 metres.

He moved fast, legs pumping in the morning light in a way that made Catherine realise she had not bothered the gym for quite some time. She made a note to think about it at a more convenient time.

She had chosen her vantage point well. He moved past her, altering his trajectory to an outermost track. Catherine could see the scowl on his face, his dark hair lank with sweat, bouncing in time with the rhythm of his feet. He seemed to be mouthing something. It was only as he passed within twenty metres that she could hear him chanting, 'Win, win, win.'

Shiloh doubled back towards the soccer fields to his north, crossing Dawson Street. Catherine waited until he was out of sight before doubling back herself to Victoria Street. She could see his trajectory and drove into the car park of the local football ground. Hiding the Vespa behind the tennis court she swapped the helmet for the tweed cap. She was about to move towards the street when she saw him slowing his run, two hundred metres away from her, bending as if to relieve a stitch. As he did this Catherine moved behind a dumpster and watched. He breathed deeply and then began walking towards the Alex G. Gillon Oval.

Catherine again exchanged hats and mounted the Vespa. Less than a minute's driving later she was hidden by the rise of the ground for spectators to watch the game. Catherine climbed a small fence of bluestone and inched her way up the rise, squatting to keep from sight. Reaching into her handbag, she pulled out her small binoculars. Shiloh appeared to be doing some sort of martial arts *kata*. She could see he was fit and flexible if the high kicks were anything to go by. Shiloh's moves increased in their intensity and Catherine gasped as she watched him moving his arms as though slashing someone's throat.

She suddenly felt sick, but continued to watch him. Then her mobile tweeted. She looked down to read the text message: it was Boris asking her to bring him a latte when she came home. Catherine turned the phone to silent.

When she looked up Shiloh had disappeared. Catherine put down the binoculars, taking in the whole field and finding no sign. She brought them back to her eyes and scanned the deserted grandstand. After a second she saw movement.

On the topmost row of grandstand seats, Shiloh sat, moving very slowly. All she could see was his silhouette, and he was laughing.

Catherine's gut churned. Had he been playing with her? She stayed still, mentally checking if the sun could have shone off her binocular glass. The sun was behind her. If he had seen her, it wasn't because of that.

He moved off his seat towards the grandstand balcony. As he moved into the light Catherine's worries died. Tears ran down his wide face. He looked to the horizon as more sobs racked him.

Catherine, mesmerised, could feel her feet going numb underneath her. She shifted her position and knelt behind the trunk of a peppercorn tree. After a few more minutes Shiloh ceased crying and moved over to his discarded jacket and took out a small black and white pouch, from which he took out tobacco, papers and what she assumed was marijuana. He rolled a small joint and smoked it.

Catherine watched him sit in the grandstand for just over fifteen minutes. She checked her watch and realised it was time to go. An interesting morning, but not worth postponing breakfast for any further.

'You been to many funerals?'

'Twenty one.'

'You know how many funerals you've been to?'

'I'm an exceedingly diligent person, Boris.'

Boris and Catherine were in Boris' car, travelling the short distance to the funeral of someone neither of them had met while she was alive. A community radio station warbled in the background as Catherine applied make-up, using the mirror on the back of the sunshade. She was aware of the toothpaste that was in her handbag and how far away it was from her tingling, hot, left buttock. Boris, as usual, was in a good mood.

'Have you calmed down sufficiently after reading the paper?'

'I never lose my temper Boris, as well you know. I was simply annoyed by the inaccurate reportage of the case.'

'The bloke you threw the fork at may disagree.'

'I wasn't throwing it at him, he was just unfortunately on the trajectory. Besides, that was not me losing my temper; I was perfectly aware of my actions.'

'You were perfectly aware of screaming obscenities and hurling the fork across a cafe?'

'As aware of that as I'm aware that you're beginning to get my goat, dear Boris.'

'Thank Christ there's no cutlery on hand.'

'This club lock looks useful. Even though it's some kind of relic.'

'Are you itchy?'

Catherine stopped moving in her seat. The flower was giving her hell, as it had all night.

'Hush, Boris. You never clean this car. There probably are pygmy tribes living in it. The Dalai Lama would fidget.'

They sat in silence after that. There was a song about an insect playing low on the radio. Catherine decided the situation was intolerable. She reached into her bag and squeezed toothpaste on to her forefinger. She waited until Boris' head was craning to see oncoming traffic to the right and stuffed her hand into her underpants. The relief was almost immediate. As she sat back in her seat she realised Boris was looking at her, a huge smile on his face. Catherine was mortified, and then he spoke.

'I just remembered there's a *Babylon Five* double episode on telly tonight.'

She couldn't help it, in the relief. She kissed him on the cheek. He looked startled.

'You all right?'

'Just happy to be alive.'

Boris mumbled something about never getting a girlfriend if she kept doing that.

'Sorry dear, just a little extra *joie de vivre* this morning.'

'Fork throwing and now affection. I'm never bored around you.'

Catherine, whose mood was much improved, ignored this and began speaking broadly about witchcraft. 'It seems to me, Boris, that a fear of witches comes from an innate discomfort certain people have with women having power. Many of the witches burned in the dark ages were midwives or medicine women. The Church was terrified of the power these women held in the community, so they were taken down, tortured, drowned and burned. This was supported often by women as much as men. It seems to fill a need in society. Which leads me to my question: why are you afraid of us?'

Boris changed gears. 'Me being?'

'Society at large'

'And you being?'

'Powerful women.'

'Right. While I must point out that I'm not afraid of you, it could have something to do with throwing forks.'

'You're not even interested in helping, are you Boris?'

'I'm driving, Catherine.'

'It's eleven. Let's catch a bit of the news.'

'They don't have news on this station.'

'Yes I know,' Catherine twisted the radio dial: 'Don't worry, four minutes of a commercial station won't turn you into a banker.'

Boris winced. 'You say that like it doesn't happen.'

'We're all products of our experience.'

'Divided by our genetics and multiplied by the country we were born into.'

'Oh shush dear, you'll give yourself a headache.'

She found the station.

'*Cassandra Pierce, the young real estate agent found murdered in an East Brunswick alley on Wednesday morning, will be buried today. Police are yet to charge anyone with her murder. In sport, Carlton have had their premiership hopes—*'

Catherine killed the radio.

'Wow, it was the lead story.'

'I'm glad they didn't list the occult items found near the body,' Catherine said.

'Speaking of occult, did you ever point out to Melissa that she was in a dangerous profession?'

'I did,' Catherine replied. 'Though I don't mean witchcraft. I warned her about chasing fame. Especially the way she's gone about it. I mean, how easy do you want to make it for people to dislike you? I couldn't believe the stuff she'd written in those blogs.'

'What's her music like?'

'Slightly better than her blogging. But lots of people like it, and lots more read her blog.'

'You're not a follower then?'

'Neither online or off, dear.'

'Hmm,' Boris' voice dropped as they turned into Sydney Road and saw the throng of people outside the church. There was a big crowd of mourners with a smattering of journalists in dark suits standing solemnly on the sidelines and cameramen set up either side of the church stairs.

'May nothing ever happen so terrible as to give us a filmed funeral,' Boris said, looking around as they arrived at the church.

'Are you attempting poetry?'

'Funerals make me romantic.'

'Arguable point.'

He turned to her and spoke between his teeth. 'That girl's looking at me.'

Catherine pretended to sneeze as she checked. 'Yes, dear. I think she might be.'

Boris did not look back. 'She looked pretty. Was she?'

'Yes, long dark hair, somewhat interesting smile, dark eyes. What are you going to do about it?'

'After the funeral?'

'Hmm, I think she just looked at you again, she's gone now.'

Boris beamed, looking towards the doors. He ran a hand through his thick, somewhat dishevelled hair. 'Feeling good boss.'

'Yes, perhaps next time a girl looks at you, talk to her, don't whisper intently to me. Women hate that kind of thing.'

As if by conspiracy, Catherine walked between two people and almost square into the still form of Detective Kenneth Williams.

'Hello, Catherine.'

'I thought you would be working.'

'I am.'

'Glad to see you're looking beyond Melissa,' said Catherine, unconsciously critiquing the various hats worn by mourners. Behind her Boris smiled cheerfully.

Williams covered his heart and Catherine wondered if he was feigning offence, but he was just checking his cigarette packet.

'Routine. All kinds of people come to funerals.'

'We're not doing that again.'

Williams gave a meaningful look, but said nothing more and found his way to three other men in the uniform suits of plainclothes police. Boris put an arm around Catherine.

'He really dislikes you, doesn't he?'

'No, I just disappointed him once.'

'Life's funny, isn't it?'

'I know. Personally, I find me delightful.'

Boris looked towards the front of the church. A couple in their fifties stood together surrounded by friends. There was nothing that identified them as the parents of Cassandra so much as the pulsating grief that emanated from them. It was in their straight stance, the way their shoulders worked against a hidden weight, the forced smiles and the eyes that stared deep into the ground.

Asher stood close by, dressed in black. Looking as much samurai as mourner. Beside him, Shiloh, in a dark brown shirt and what looked suspiciously like black jeans. Worse still, he was wearing a fedora. Catherine's dislike increased. The fedora renaissance, which had been a quaint idea years earlier, was now just a blight on the hat-wearing world. Nearly always worn by a man, despite the fact they were intended for women. Just because Harrison Ford had pulled it off in the eighties, didn't mean everyone could now. They were a disappointment with a cherry on top, and they were everywhere.

'Hey,' Boris whispered.

'Hey.'

'That's the guy.'

'Which one, what guy?' Catherine monotoned.

'Guy next to Asher, wearing one of those hats you hate. He's the one who was stalking Frawley.'

'That's Shiloh, Asher's brother.'

Boris did a good job of making himself smaller as he continued, 'I suspect he took the pictures of me yesterday.'

'I think you should make yourself scarce.'

'I'll be at the office. I think we've found suspect number one.'

'I'll see if he smells like a kid's party.'

As Boris melted into the background, Catherine walked inside the church, which was filled with light, the old stained glass windows illuminating rows of dark wooden pews.

Catherine found herself a place near the rear. She counted six hats and had found them all pleasing, aside from Shiloh's, though none of her own design. Standing for the opening hymn, she placed her hands in front of her and looked solemn. She scanned the room as the priest began his sad refrain. Those who hadn't found seats were standing at the back or on the edges of the pews. The congregation was a mix of races and ages, predominantly Cassandra's contemporaries.

Cassandra's sister Anna moved to the pulpit, shuffled a few pages and breathed deeply before looking at the congregation.

'What is a stone, a pair of scissors, the sound of laughter? What is a life lived full and cut short? What is a most cherished love and a greatest regret? All of these are my sister. All of these are Cassandra. Your words will ring in the darkness and your smile remains immortal in photo frames and within my heart. You touched the lives of thousands with your smile. You shone brighter than most. Though it made sense that light would not shine forever.' Her voice broke and she took two quick, deep breaths. Catherine looked around, there were more tears now.

Anna continued: 'I remember you best as the sister just a few feet away from me. I remember the space between our beds as we were growing up. When the lights were turned off and we would talk as sisters do, I remember feeling like the entire space was full of our words, laughter and love. That was a space no one else could touch.

'In the past days I have thought about that space more and more. About how it could seem that there was a universe between us, and yet with just a few words from you that space could just be so small again.

'Seeing you in love these past few years gave me so much joy. I know my parents and I looked forward to your children and all the things that now are not to be. You did not deserve your fate. No one would. We will remember you and your light and your smile. I will hold you with me forever.'

She stood on the altar, taller than her sister Cassandra, taller than Boris, for that matter. She wore muted clothes and her hair was short. She spoke her poetic words with a thick voice. The heart-broken victim of a horrible crime.

The church smelled of flowers and incense. Cologne. Catherine could smell aftershave in unusual proportions, a haze of forced olfactory charm. She suspected the culprits were the immaculately dressed men of varying ages that dotted the congregation, looking perfectly pressed in the manner of real estate workers everywhere.

There were muted references to Cassandra's past. Much discussion of a lust for life and *Dead Poets' Society* inspired *joie de vivre*. Of rowing team triumphs and being the last on the dance floor. Some spoke of regret they had not kept in touch.

Catherine had been told Cassandra liked to win. Was that part of the reason behind not keeping friends? Catherine had friends that had gone by the wayside because of Catherine's dislike of ambition. There were times even Mel only held on by the skin of her teeth. Or was it more simple? Was Cassandra's relationship keeping her from friends? A job, a partner, many found this enough and stopped going out as much. Catherine breathed deeply and as her lungs filled with cologne, she imagined such a life. To each their own, but it sounded like hell to her.

Afterwards people spilled out of the church and past the cameras. The funeral party had driven away after a few minutes of people weeping and embracing, while others looked blankly at each other. Catherine headed for the brothers Marr. Asher stood deep in conversation with a stunning, tall, blonde woman who kept pushing her face into his shoulder. Catherine tried her best to ignore it, but her ear kept twitching the way it did when she threw forks. Shiloh was standing nearby smoking and scowling.

'Lovely service,' she began.

He looked at her over his sunglasses, took a drag on his cigarette, blew the smoke near her. He stayed silent. Catherine smiled indulgently. 'Sorry, am I breaking your view of yourself? I could leave you to smoke and pose?'

He was silent for a few more seconds. Catherine was about to give up when he spoke. 'We've exchanged a few words, I've told you where to go; why bother with small talk?'

Catherine smiled breezily. 'Because one day we will both be dead. Because what separates us from other species is we both know it. The only weapons we have against this impending doom are drugs, humour and small talk. It's too early for the first two. So: lovely service.'

His lips twitched, suppressing a grin. 'Yes, they painted her picture well.'

All of Shiloh's previous hostility had moved into a detached strangeness.

'Why aren't you going with the funeral party?'

Shiloh exhaled smoke towards the dilapidated steeple of the church and nodded at his brother. 'They weren't married. I needed a smoke.' He removed his sunglasses, returning to his usual habit of creepy eye contact. 'They never mentioned just how selfish she could be, but I suppose they wouldn't, would they?'

Catherine digested this for a second. 'Very candid. It's nice to meet someone whose love of an individual doesn't cloud their honesty.'

'Do you mind me talking like that? I didn't realise you knew her.'

'I didn't, and I don't mind.' As she spoke she pretended to look at her shoes and inhaled deeply. She normally wouldn't have broken eye contact, but she needed to know if he was last night's driver. She smelt cigarette smoke, marijuana, mid-shelf aftershave and what could possibly be bacon balls eaten in the last 12 hours, but no sparklers. That said, the projectile had been thrown twelve hours earlier. Even a poor criminal could change clothes.

When she looked back he was smiling. He enjoyed outstaring her.

'Asher tells me you work for the witch.'

'I work for myself, but yes. By the way, do you know a man called Marcus Frawley?'

'Worked with Cassandra?'

'Yes. I was wondering if you knew whether they got along?'

'Ever met Frawley?'

'Only once.'

'Nobody gets along with Frawley, he's always pointing the finger.' Shiloh's smile had become vulpine. Catherine was disappointed, as she always did when people tried to intimidate her.

They were interrupted by Asher's arm curling around his brother's shoulder. 'So sorry Catherine, I have to steal him. We have to go to the cemetery.' He gave a sad grin, then looked up. 'See you at the wake perhaps?'

'Thanks for the chat, Shiloh. Let me know if you ever need a hand.' Asher pulled him away faster after that, but Shiloh turned and started laughing, just for a moment.

When Boris left the church he felt a change in the air that was not all to do with temperature. A few TV crews glanced at him as he walked past before going back to their phones. Boris figured he had at least forty minutes to search for an Audi. He was moving off when a beautiful young woman came up to him with a voice recorder. 'Do you mind, sir?'

'Not at all.' Boris gave his best smile. This was a moment he would describe in their wedding speech.

'Given the heinous crime, are you in favour of the murderer facing the death penalty?'

Boris sagged; true love had died once again. He fought stupefaction for a full three seconds before he spluttered: 'Are you even a journalist?'

'I'm from *Christian Weekly Times*.'

He stared at her. 'I don't think Jesus was into capital punishment by the end. Dickhead.' He pushed past.

She stared back like a righteous angel of vengeance. Boris noticed she seemed to dance a little as she walked back to her clique.

He hated doing that. For the next three hours he would replay the scene, being more polite, being witty, and engaging in a dialogue about sensationalist journalism and the pros and cons of capital punishment. Or the version where he just stayed silent, and gave her a look that showed his contempt and possible virility.

Suddenly feeling about a thousand years old, he scanned each side of the street; the plan was do a block at a time in circles crossing over the church. While he walked and looked, he thought of the nature of all punishment as excessive. Punishment by definition had to be excessive to negate the thrill of the crime. Death by the state had always filled him with dread. How easily humans would judge that another should die. We would say it was done for a greater good and we would say that it was right. Killing in the name of society, and the state, never admitting our hope that by killing another we warded ourselves from our own day of reckoning.

As he turned away from Sydney Road he saw three black cars. Two were the wrong make and one was an Audi but with the personalised numberplate, *BOOT5IE*. Boris checked the screws – no sign of a recent change. The windows were tinted. Definitely not the right car. If someone could change number plates and get a car tinted to avoid detection, they would probably make a better projectile than the one used last night.

He moved on. The block was wide and industrial. The groans of forklifts from the warehouses on the other side of the road were interrupted by the sound of children playing at a nearby primary school. He peered through the windows of a black BMW with similar plates to what he sought, but all he got was a shout and a look from a nearby heavy having a smoke.

Boris waved in a way that said, 'Hello, I just love Beemers don't you?' and moved on.

He had gone around the block and was almost alongside the church again when he saw it. Across Sydney Road at the end of a side street, parked in the shade of paperbark trees. Even before Boris checked the number plate he knew it was the one. It just felt right. He was halfway across the road and there was the number-plate in all its glory: XRZ 546, Black Audi, newish model. The inside was unremarkable. There was a newspaper over the passenger seat and a takeaway coffee cup in the cup holder. An invoice for a mechanic lay on the dashboard. Dated for yesterday. Whomever it was had got the car serviced to throw a bottle at him. Nice to know there was such consideration in the world.

The church service would go at least another half hour. He checked the street but could see no possible parking spots; everything was full due to the funeral. Returning to his car, he slid into the seat and found that he had parked just a few metres too far to be able to see that part of Michael Street.

Formulating a plan C, he found an old blanket that he'd packed for a picnic some time ago. He was sure there had been a pillow in there at some stage but he couldn't place it, though he found a trusty straw hat. Taking the blanket back down the street, he nuzzled into a warehouse doorway, covering his face with the hat. Play to your strengths when it comes to camouflage. Boris had always suspected he had potential as a vagrant and now was his time to shine. He had a good clear line of sight to the Audi and the gates of the church.

Fifteen minutes of studiously not sleeping later he began to hear sounds of group discussion from across the road. Boris wondered idly if Catherine would notice him and accuse him of skiving. He saw someone move towards the car. The smirk said it all. It made sense; it was worn by the kind of man who might think that sparklers would throw Catherine off the scent. The kind of would-be heavy who could be intimidated by a wordless stranger in a Brunswick pub. It was a man who could even be stalked by a lover of plastic flowers – Marcus Frawley.

'Well that makes much more sense,' muttered Boris as Frawley drove away.

8

DNA discussions relax me – it's being half banana that gets me through some days.
~ Boris Shakhovskoy

The wake took up most of the large courtyard of the Penny Black Hotel. The clouds that had gathered after the funeral had dissipated and now the sun shone brightly past the umbrellas and on to dark wooden tables densely covered with glasses of champagne and beer. Photos of Cassandra and her family and friends lined the room. The effect was almost haphazard, yet beautiful; Cassandra was in each corner and on every table, filling the room. Catherine chatted to a group of girls who had not seen Cassandra since high school. They were a mixed bag of married, single, happy and bitter. One mindlessly fondled a pregnant belly and the others held champagne flutes. None had kept up with Cassandra 'as much as we'd have liked', and there was a hint of a long-ago dispute involving someone's boyfriend. Catherine asked if they had ever met Asher.

'Oh, yes. He's lovely, he always included the old friends when he could.'

'It was just that Cassie was so busy, work, you know.'

Catherine broke from the group when she saw her chance with Cassandra's sister, Anna. She was easy to see, standing about six foot two in her heels. 'Anna, I'm Catherine. I just wanted say how sorry I am.'

Anna's head bobbed and she smiled, already experienced at receiving condolences with grace.

'Thank you. Did you know my sister well?'

'Not as well as I'd have liked. Your eulogy was very moving. Do you write?'

'A bit of poetry. It was a hard thing to write. She and I were close.'

'A most cherished love and greatest regret,' Catherine quoted. 'When did you last see her?'

Anna Pierce looked tired suddenly; tears welled in her eyes. 'Six months ago.'

Catherine nodded, preserving Anna's silence. After a pause, the tall girl continued: 'It never seemed quite so long before.'

Again Catherine nodded. A familiar old sting of memory had tugged at her during Anna's eulogy. She sipped her wine while Anna continued.

'We were rivals for a time when we were teenagers, but after, I gave up. She could win all the time, I didn't care, I just wanted to be sisters.'

'It's too much, isn't it?' Catherine's hand rested lightly on Anna's forearm. She was unsure even why she said that, but it hit a nerve. Silent tears rolled down Anna's cheeks.

Anna's father was suddenly upon them, holding his daughter as more sobs wracked her body. Catherine made eye contact and gave a wan smile that was returned in kind. She left them there. Left them to heal. She had all the information she would likely get, and to stay would be ghoulish.

As she moved toward the door, a movement caught her eye. On the opposite wall, across the vacant stage, Catherine saw a man move quickly in the room backstage, behind a wooden door with glass panels. She moved across the stage and then stopped. Asher had his back to her, while Shiloh pointed a finger in his face. Shiloh seemed to be shouting, but Catherine could not hear the words. She moved to the left, out of sight of the door and closer, and bent down as though attending to her shoe while peering through the glass. She still could not make out the words but the passion in Shiloh's voice was unmistakable. Then Catherine saw Shiloh throw himself at Asher, with hands outstretched, his fingers like claws.

Catherine did not see Asher move, but suddenly Shiloh was on the floor, his hat landing behind him. Asher pivoted and seemed poised to strike again, but Catherine saw his lips move and then he raised a hand, as if to quiet his brother.

He knelt down, very calmly, and held out his hand to help Shiloh regain his footing. Shiloh stood and fell against his brother. Shiloh's face was buried in Asher's shoulder and they rocked against each other.

Then Asher turned and looked directly at her. He winked.

A moment later they walked out together. Asher held out a hand. 'Thanks for looking out for us. Must you go?'

'I think it's best. I never met her.'

Shiloh moved towards the bar without looking at them. Catherine watched him go.

'What was that about?'

'Family and funerals. Always hard. Just old wounds and such.' Asher walked away before she could stop him.

Catherine left the pub for the bank next door and asked to speak with Kirsten. The teller asked the nature of her business.

'I believe she is a real wizard with finance. I'd like her to work her magic,' Catherine replied.

The clerk looked puzzled, but moved inside and a few minutes later Catherine's hand was gripped by a stunning woman, aged about forty-five, in a dark grey power suit. She had lush blonde hair down to her shoulders and could have pulled off a pillbox like the great Jackie O herself.

Kirsten Hazlewood, branch financial consultant, made assured eye contact past unframed glasses and possessed a poise that Catherine found contagious. She felt herself standing straighter as she was ushered into a small office. 'Catherine, what can I help you with?'

'I'm a friend of Melissa Zamansky. She sent me here because of your special talents.'

Kirsten closed the door before she answered. 'So I take it you're not going to ask about how to effectively build a portfolio of flexible but high-yielding bonds?'

'No, I want to talk about magic.'

Kirsten looked at Catherine as if she were a maths problem. Catherine was suddenly feeling almost naked, and the hairs on the back of her neck bristled.

'Is Melissa in some kind of trouble?' Kirsten asked distractedly.

'That's why I'm here.'

The look continued, as if she was being scanned. Catherine moved beyond momentary intimidation to her natural state of curiosity. 'Like what you see?'

'I was looking at your aura. You drink too much, your aura is everywhere. You're enjoying it, though. Does that worry you?'

'What?'

'How much you like filling an empty tin?' Catherine gripped her handbag harder than she would have liked at such a question.

'I'm not here to talk about me.'

'No. Melissa sent you to me. Interesting. Catherine, I am a busy woman, I will give you five minutes, so go: What do you need to know?'

'The girl who was recently killed near here had been staring at a wheat sheaf. Her three fingers were cut off. I couldn't see any other signs of rites, but it seemed occult.'

'You can look this up on the internet, why come to me?'

'I want to know one thing: what could have been the benefit to Melissa to do this crime.'

'You think she did it?'

'No, but I need to know why someone would do such a thing. Generally people kill for a reason.'

Kirsten pushed an invisible out of place hair back behind her ear. 'As you can probably guess, blood is a powerful conduit of power. Tell me, was the blood concentrated in one particular direction, or did it look like it had been harvested?'

'No, aside from the sheaf and the fingers, it seemed like a straight-up murder, if there is such a thing.'

'So it was scattering of blood to the earth? Pagan worship is based around living in harmony with the earth and the seasons, and the wheat sheaf is certainly a pagan sign around equinox, when this happened. The sheaf represents the harvest coming and the gifts of the coming season. So here's the kicker for you: anyone who practices Wicca and was planning on killing a girl as a sacrifice would not have done it on that date – equinox is when things are in balance and it's a day when a witch will attempt to balance herself. She may fast, may give ritual thanks, but to murder on a day such as equinox flies in the face of the Wiccan tradition. If this was done for magical purposes it was done by someone who has inverted the religion and is looking to abominable means for power.'

'So to answer my short question: there was no benefit to Melissa.'

'None. Melissa is a fool who wants to be in magazines, but has some talent for magic. She's committed to the path. I can see no benefit to her pursuit of the path in this act. Now, if you'll excuse me, I have a national phone hook-up in two minutes.'

Shortly afterwards Catherine sat on her favourite park bench, staring at the afternoon clouds and idly scratching her itchy rump. Resolved that Melissa had nothing to gain by the killing but jail time, Catherine went through every piece of information the morning had given her regarding Cassandra Guadalupe Pierce. Funerals were difficult, as were sisters. Must call Cynthia one of these days. Must go and work on the brim pieces. Must call Boris now, though it was Asher she really wanted to speak to.

She thought of the Marr brothers at the funeral, fighting and then embracing. Compared to a sister relationship, she really knew little of how brothers worked; only that they so often seemed to have either won or lost some genetic roll of the dice. What makes men like Shiloh and Asher so different, however alike? What must it be like to have a brother as in control as Asher or as difficult as Shiloh?

Then again there was the problem of having a brilliant parent. Her own father was so brilliant in his field and yet he remained as humble a man as any. Probably why her boyfriends never quite cut the proverbial.

She was jolted out of the daydream by her mobile, a private number. Catherine heard the sound of trucks and cars, a payphone perhaps. There was a cough. Catherine rolled the dice.

'Asher?'

There was another cough, and then: 'Yes, Catherine. Hi, it's me.' The park bench suddenly seemed warmer at the idea of him. 'I was wondering if you were free, right now? Would you happen to be at a loose end, as we speak?'

Catherine felt a stirring near her lily. She had forgotten that she'd left her phone number on their answering machine.

'Aren't you at your lover's wake?' A girl had her decency after all.

'Yes I am. But I can't stay, it's too much. I think I know who killed her.'

'Meet me at the overpass near Brunswick station in fifteen minutes.'

Boris considered taking his car to the Glasgow Palace, but decided that he may need to drive further. He parked in the lengthening shadows on Sydney Road, just across from Jewel Real Estate. Yesterday he had heard Frawley organise a rendezvous at his office at 6pm, if it were to still occur. He checked his watch – 5.15 – he had time to find a vantage point.

As he opened his car door, three cyclists moved past; two lycrapaths and a hippie mother with a child on a seat behind her. They were the only vehicles travelling south for blocks. The traffic in the other direction was banked up, with four trams heading north marking out points in the kilometre-long jam. Boris got out of the car and thought about bicycles. Everyone in Melbourne was using them these days. He had read an article last week stating they had outsold car sales for the past five years running. Boris tried to work out when was the last time he really needed his car for a trip that couldn't have been cycled and whether he could shed the pounds quicker going on two wheels.

As he crossed the street, he was buzzed by another lycra-dad with earphones in and sunglasses on. The cyclist didn't say anything but grunted at Boris with a special kind of contempt before kicking on at a rate of knots. Shooting past the immobile cars. Boris watched him go; his lycra was a puce blur.

'I could never be one of them.' Cycling seemed to be suffering the same problems as God and Collingwood – the hardcore were ruining it for everyone else.

He saw Frawley's empty car outside his office. Boris wondered why he had not gone to the wake. Boris had never been to a funeral where he hadn't moved on to the wake for a sandwich or three, but Frawley had gone straight back to work. Boris had already decided that he and Frawley had a different take on life. The blinds were drawn at the office. Boris walked back towards his car. Yesterday must have been an amazingly bad day for Frawley. As low as Boris had felt being stalked, at least he wasn't being double stalked. It didn't justify throwing a lemonade bottle filled with low grade explosives at him, but nonetheless Boris' empathy gave a quiet twinge.

Boris walked past his car and found a suitable vantage point. With yesterday's cafe closed he went to the Vietnamese restaurant next door. He chose a spot in the middle of the room with a good enough view that he wouldn't miss much, but far enough back from the window that he wouldn't be so easily seen. This would be where a real investigator would order tea and stare until something happened, ignoring the wonderful smells around him because he was focused, so focused on the task at hand. This was where Boris was not a real investigator. He ordered fried quail and imperial rice, whispering a prayer of thanks to Catherine for his investigative stipend that made such indulgences possible.

As he chewed prawn crackers, he watched employees of Jewel Real Estate file out slowly. For a few seconds a tram blocked his view. When his view was clear again he felt certain that he had missed nothing of importance. His eyes fixed on the buildings doors even as quail arrived, he picked it up in two fingers and contemplated its frailty as he took a bite.

He burned his mouth and his jerking hand spilt his water. His eyes watered and he made a sound like a small dying robot. A Vietnamese family in the corner subdued their small daughter who had almost fallen out of her chair laughing. His cool nonchalance had evaporated, his contemplation done. He smiled at them weakly as the mother crossed the room and offered him a fistful of napkins, even rubbing his back a little. It occurred to him that Sam Spade would never have done that. As his mouth cooled he consoled himself with imperial rice and dreamt cooling thoughts. Not everyone needed to be a tough guy.

At 6.09 a familiar figure passed the window of the restaurant and Boris almost dropped his chopsticks. He swore in a high voice. Yesterday's intimidating presence in black, now identified as Shiloh Marr, was on the other side of the glass. Only the four-millimetre glass window was now protecting Boris from discovery. Thankfully Shiloh was facing the other way, watching traffic before crossing Sydney Road. At the door of the estate agent's office Shiloh took his phone out and made a call. Marcus Frawley appeared at the door promptly and let him in. Frawley took a look both ways and then disappeared into the building.

Hurriedly paying after abandoning his meal, Boris crossed the road. He moved as fast as his food-filled body could carry him and leaned against the wall just to the right of where he hoped Frawley's office was. The blind was drawn, but down on his haunches, he could see a few centimetres in the top corner of the room. He wondered if a view of a superman figure on top of a filing cabinet would crack this case open for Catherine? Hardly. He could just note the times in and out and then go for a beer and wait for Catherine to call in. Then he heard a door slam inside the building, followed by muffled voices. Frawley's reedy tone pierced through glass.

'I don't know why you need all this cloak and dagger rubbish. Just pay me and it goes away.'

'Oh, I'm sure you would, Marcus, but then I think a little while down the line, you'd pop up again. I just have that feeling about you.' Shiloh's voice was matter-of-fact.

'I think you'd find me very professional. Didn't I prove myself last night?'

'Oh, very helpful. She seemed absolutely terrified today when she—' A tram rolled past and Boris missed the end of the sentence. Shiloh was still speaking when the background noise subsided. 'He's powerful, he's ruthless and he'll get it done no matter what you print.'

'I'm just doing what's right, mate. She gave me that folder because she thought something might happen to her.'

'She gave you that folder to piss someone off. And don't dare insinuate that we've got something to do with her death. She was going to be my sister-in-law.'

A couple walked past Boris, staring at him as he crouched by the window. He smiled at them and theatrically tied his shoelace. They moved on. Frawley was pushing hard for a close.

'It's simple then. I'll give you the files if you give me the cash.'

'Like I said, Marcus, I don't think we can trust you. I think you need to show your loyalty before any money changes hands.'

'This is bull. I could just send everything away now. To my lawyer, my boss, the papers. What do you think of that?'

There was a low laugh and Shiloh said something Boris couldn't hear.

Frawley's voice got higher in pitch. 'Don't play tough, you just said you had nothing to do with it.'

There were more murmurs, followed by a crash that made Boris jump.

'Just get out.' Frawley cried out, seemingly in pain.

'You understand, Marcus, I'm just a soldier. Doing what I'm told. And if someone says ill about a soldier's father, well. It gets heated, doesn't it? I'll be in touch.'

'My money.' Frawley groaned. Boris had heard men groan like that – it usually involved lying on the ground after someone had hurt you.

'A test later Marcus, father loves a good test.'

'Get off.' Frawley sounded close to hysteria. Shiloh was almost salesman-like in his smooth delivery.

'It's about power, Marcus. Everyone wants a powerful friend, and my father has it in spades. It's in my blood, you see. Blood.'

There was a further crash. Boris figured Shiloh had made his point and was coming out.

Boris moved quickly up the street, sprinting for about thirty metres before ducking into a pub. What he had heard raised more questions than it gave answers, but one certainty was that Boris – if he could help it – did not want to get on the bad side of Shiloh Marr. Boris looked back; Shiloh was striding across the road. He hailed a cab, opened the door, then paused and looked up the street towards the bar. Boris ducked beneath a couch, counted to five and then rose to watch Shiloh slide into the taxi's back seat.

'You right, mate?' asked a concerned punter.

'Yeah mate,' replied Boris, reassuringly. 'I'm bloody marvellous.'

Fourteen minutes and twelve anticipatory seconds later, Catherine and Asher stood on the overpass of the Upfield train line. Catherine shivered with cold. Worse, the drop in temperature was irritating the flower on her posterior. Asher, for his part, was quiet after an initial "hello". They looked north, watching the light reflect off a thousand west-facing windows.

'Did you make a speech?'

'Yes,' he said. 'It didn't go very well. She deserved better. Then I rang you and left. Hey, are you cold?'

He began to remove his jacket.

'No, I'm fine', Catherine lied. Nice that he thought of it, though. In her mind, an abacus moved a bead in Asher's favour.

'I'm sorry to call you out here. Sorry, I'm so awkward. I'm usually not like this; and I usually don't babble like an idiot,' he smiled a little at this, gave a sideways glance and seemed relieved that Catherine was also smiling. 'Catherine, I think Cassandra may have been killed by Marcus Frawley.'

Catherine nodded slowly while she adjusted her suspicions. She had been enjoying the sound of his voice. It had a lovely tenor quality, distracting her. 'Why do you say that?'

'I barely know him, but Cassandra had talked about how much he hated her. Then he gave me this look at the church today.' He looked at her. 'It's weak I know, but I just wanted to say it out loud and you seemed the person to do that with. I just don't think that your friend Melissa could overpower Cassandra. She doesn't seem that strong.'

They walked for a while, northwards on the bike path. Catherine was keen to keep him talking.

'What about the fingers?'

He shrugged; Catherine noticed his muscular shoulders even under his jacket. His face was drawn in sadness. 'Yeah, it was quite a jinx. Doesn't make sense with the Frawley thing.' He breathed out hard and stopped walking, resting his hand on a wooden fence that blocked the bike path from the train. The graffiti on the opposite walls was beautiful, vivid, elaborate shapes and ciphers of colour that no one over the age of sixteen had a hope of interpreting. Made her think of the things you don't notice losing as you age.

He turned to her. 'You don't think she did it, do you?'

She was back in the moment. 'No. This thing is a set up.' She watched him chew his lip and his neck muscles rippled.

'Does that make you wonder if it was me?' There was still enough light to see the weariness in his face. He looked completely vulnerable.

'I can't see it.'

He sighed and kept walking. 'I can't tell you what it means to hear you say that.'

'Though you can obviously handle yourself. I saw the way you brought Shiloh down.'

'Shiloh could have me any day of the week in a fight except for one thing: I'm his big brother.' He made a face and held his hands like a boogieman.

Catherine smiled. 'Politics hits even the most enlightened families then.'

'Oh yes, we all know our place. Buddha says if you know, just know.'

The mental abacus moved against him. There were ten kinds of hippies, and Catherine didn't like nine of them. 'What else have you got on Frawley?'

'Nothing. Just that Cassandra didn't like him, he didn't like Cassandra. He gave me a scowl at her funeral... I want to know what happened that night.'

'So you said. First tell me why you pulled your brother away from me today?'

'When?'

'Just after the funeral.'

'You intimidate him.'

Catherine tried not to show how much she liked that idea. She watched the wind blow Asher's hair. A train hooted, far away. He seemed impossibly pretty.

'I was asking him about Frawley.'

'I think it was upsetting him.'

'Why would it?'

'He was a bit highly strung today.' He looked away at the last lines of sun. She could still see him in the glow of the streetlamps from the nearby roads. His face was still, no twitches or any other signs of conflict. No signs of a straight answer, either.

'What were you fighting about at the wake?'

'Old wound. Funerals make him remember our mother.'

Catherine squared her shoulders. 'This will not work unless you're completely honest with me.'

'What do you mean?' Asher asked. 'I asked for the truth and you came. I wouldn't lie to you, you're the key.'

'You may have to work out if you want to catch your girlfriend's killer, or protect your brother.'

He looked to the sky. Whatever he was looking for, he didn't find. He just smiled at her as she rubbed her bare arms. He removed his jacket and gave it to her.

'You got a brother?'

'A sister. Cynthia.'

'Close?'

'Close enough.' His jacket smelled like a hint of cologne, the good kind, and only the faintest hint.

'Do you think Shiloh could hide something from you?'

'Not for long, he likes to get my input on most things.'

'What would he keep from you? Stalking a realtor?'

'I'm sure that is just a misunderstanding. I think he's probably thinking along the same lines as me.'

'Would that be his only motivation?'

Asher swallowed. 'Y'know I don't always trust my brother. It's horrid to say, and we are close. He's another person I really know. I think because I know him so well is why I can't completely see him through rose-coloured glasses. He's very like our father.'

'And what is he like?'

'Controlling. And unpredictable. I don't know what you know of his movement, but he's the centre of it. He's full of the spirituality of sex and worship, mostly of himself.' He flashed a grin. 'He liked to know everything that was going on and that we kept our best face on at all times.'

'Not what I had expected of the great Alexander Marr.'

'We called him Thoth.'

'Pardon?'

Now he was smiling broadly, his teeth white in the dark. 'That was his name in our house, Thoth, or very occasionally, Dad.'

'Thoth. Egyptian?' Catherine had vague memories of a man's body with the head of an ibis.

'God of wisdom and the dead, correct. My father was an amazing man, but somewhat self-important.'

'Was?' Catherine was finding it difficult not to flirt. He would look great in a felt faux-admiralty style hat. No wonder she was drawn to him. Only ten per cent of men could do that. She began walking again and he fell in step easily.

'He's declined a great deal in the past few years. The worst thing you can do as a guru is begin to believe what the disciples are telling you. Lose grip on reality.'

'Is that a trait that Shiloh shares?'

'Shiloh was very angry with Thoth. He'd been trying to win his respect for years; and Thoth has drifted further and further from what we knew. I know it's a great strain on him.'

'And you?'

'And me?'

'Are you trying to win your father's respect?'

There were a thoughtful couple of steps at this juncture. 'No, I had an easier time before, and now I'm glad he's not around. I knew he was my Dad and that was enough.'

'You didn't mourn the relationship when it changed?'

'I did for a time I guess, but then I let go. I'm glad he's happy. Even if he's far away.'

'Where is he?'

'Thailand, on a kind of permanent retreat. Though sometimes he just turns up. I never know exactly when he's in Australia until he's with us.'

'Does he know about Cassandra's death?'

'I sent an email. No reply yet, but that's not unusual. When he's deep in his teachings, things like correspondence don't take priority for him.'

'So where do the teachings come from?'

'Father's been a guru for forty years. Open your head to prahna, open your mind to love, open your wallet to my sons with their bank account, and if you're a girl...' He shrugged and looked towards the horizon.

'I feel like I've just been let into a big secret that everyone's always suspected,' Catherine said.

Asher gave a shy smile, her favourite kind. 'You haven't. I could scream this during my father's sermons, I could write it to the papers. Shiloh disagrees, thinks we should be so careful, but people will believe what they want to, that's the key. Those who think that's what the New Age is all about will agree and those who see Dad as their road to peace would just add me to their list of people who didn't understand.'

'It's all about the romance, isn't it?'

'All people want is the truth and a little magic.' Asher's hands moved in the air as if conjuring.

'And to feel like they're better than everyone who's not on the path to truth.'

He nodded. 'That's the secret ingredient.'

A bat flapped lazily above them, catching Catherine's eye and making her think momentarily of a double gin and tonic. She pushed herself back to what she could loosely call business.

'Tell me, is Shiloh always rude to women or is it just me?'

'Well, to be fair you should meet him on a week when one of his friends hasn't been murdered. He can be very unpredictable, though.'

'Does he have a history of violence?'

Asher's mouth twitched, Catherine counted three beats before he answered, 'Yes.'

'Asher, do you really think it was Marcus who killed Cassandra?'

Catherine counted under her breath. She thought she may have seen a tear fall in the newly fallen darkness, but couldn't be sure.

'I don't,' he said quietly.

Catherine nodded. 'So, you don't think it was Frawley?'

Asher put his hands on the rail, steadying himself. 'But I don't think it was Shiloh. It could have been anyone. That's why I need you.'

'You don't want to suspect him?'

'No.' He was looking at the train that was heading towards the city.

'But you want me to find out what happened?'

The train rolled past with squealing wheels and rumbling engine.

'Yeah,' he said. Catherine put her arm around him, he leaned into her. 'It takes a lot for someone to actually face what their mind is telling them. If you didn't ask now, you would be silently asking your whole life. Do you think Shiloh has it in him?'

'He loved Cassandra.'

'I'm sure he did,' Catherine said. 'Could he have killed her?'

'If he did, he was pretty amazing at acting surprised when I told him.'

'Asher, you told police that you and Shiloh spent the night at home when Cassandra was killed.'

'I lied.'

'Where were you?'

'At home.'

'Where was he?'

'He told me he was with our lawyer until midnight; from there he went to a brothel. He likes to…' he waved a hand vaguely, 'then got home about 4am.'

Catherine said nothing, though she stiffened slightly. Shiloh's alibi was a lie, which rendered Asher's the same; and her arm was still around him.

Asher continued: 'I don't like to think about it.'

'Have you been to the brothel with Shiloh?'

'Why do you ask that?'

'I want to know if it exists, or if it's just a thing he talks about when he doesn't want you to know where he is.'

'I'm sorry, I just. I haven't been there, but I've dropped him at it before. It exists. It's on Lygon Street in East Brunswick.'

'So in the same suburb Cassandra died. Do you know anyone who works there?'

'No.'

His free hand gripped the rail hard.

Catherine changed tack. 'Last night you mentioned others who may have wanted Cassandra to lose. Who?'

He inhaled deeply. 'I can't think of anyone specifically.'

'How about Thoth? You said sometimes he comes back here without telling you.'

'The way he's been there's a chance that he's moved to Mars.' He was speaking quietly. 'It's not impossible.'

'Was he ever violent towards you?'

'No.' He looked down again. 'It was to our mother.'

'I see.' Catherine decided she was going to start charging by the hour. She moved away from Asher, while he continued. 'She killed herself when I was eighteen. They had been separated a long time. I think she was still afraid of him.' He looked at her with a tear in his eye. 'What a day.'

Catherine thought of the seventeen-year-old girl mentioned in the newspaper article from thirty years earlier, about her walking bloodied down Lygon Street. The guru, it seemed could hurt people, women especially.

Despite herself she put an arm around him again. His jacket was warm and smelled like skin.

'There will be better days.'

Somehow his arms were around her waist.

'Catherine.'

His body was tight and firm and full of promise. She liked how he said her name.

His hand caressed her face, his fingers over her ears and down along her neck. He knew just how to touch a woman. Catherine felt ninety-eight per cent of her body go to him and the other two become suddenly inflamed with an itchiness that made her remember untrue alibis and murdered women.

She broke away. He stood, looking hungry and resigned.

'I'm so sorry.'

Catherine was having trouble breathing. It wasn't appropriate, but that hadn't stopped her before. But until she was sure, she couldn't; the cursed arsecheek just made it easier.

'No, don't.'

'I am.'

'Don't apologise, there's just a protocol. Even if you live your life outside convention.'

'I need you. There is nothing worse than being afraid.'

'You only say that because you have never been burned by flowers.'

9

It's easy to be good when people notice.
~ Nealamber Singh

That should have been the end of the night. It had been a lovely, well-rounded evening of intrigue and flirtation. Now all and sundry should have clocked off, gone home, maybe watched telly or read a book. Rested for another mysterious day, another twenty-four hours in which the world could upend itself for some and silently move on for most.

Yet the day was not done. Some days, like mischievous toddlers, will just kick and scream their way into the early hours no matter how many stories you read.

Catherine walked home. There was cab money in her purse, but she needed to digest what had just happened while she was anonymous and mobile. Boris had sent her a text saying he was home if she needed him. As she moved up Sydney Road and beyond, she heard Asher's voice in her head. First implicating Frawley, then speaking of his father like a spectre who would one day devour him. The way he had possibly already devoured Shiloh. Then she remembered him saying that he knew his father and that was enough. Sophocles would have loved the Marr family.

Further to this Catherine wondered at the decline of the Chinese restaurant in suburban Melbourne. The Greens party – would they ever be able to succeed anywhere aside from the inner city while protecting the bush? And whether the Palace would be open long enough for her to down a gin with Boris and nut it out. As she passed the spot where Alice had cursed her, she blew a raspberry.

At Albion Street, Catherine gazed at the inside of the Palace only to see chairs on tables and Leon sitting by himself watching the news. While Catherine was reasonably sure that he would pour her a drink, she decided to leave him to it and go home. There was always the lure of listening to Cole Porter tracks on the balcony and staring at the night sky, or doing thorough and diligent research on The Shining Way and similar groups or even doing some much needed catch-up on her actual job – those hats just wouldn't make themselves.

Or, she mused as she climbed the tan tiled stairs of her townhouse, she could read the mysterious envelope which was propped against her doorstep with her name scribbled on it in red capital letters. She noted as she opened the door that there was no marking of delivery, and gave a mental high five to Minty who passed by on her way to some night-time cat ablutions. Once inside, she put her bag on the ornate dark-wood hat stand and opened the envelope. The paper was like papyrus, thick and grainy, with a message typed in black ink.

There are many paths to peace; many can only be walked by those willing to leave all baggage behind. Your money, your pride, your family are all burdens that you will need to put aside if you are readying yourself for the "shadow path" which despite its name, will bring you to light. Only the boldest take this way, for it is filled with a beauty that will take your eyes and a sensory experience beyond the physical. It is the Father who can show you the wisdom, but there are many Fathers.

For those willing to take this path, an ecstasy awaits that is beyond flesh. Indeed flesh, however lovely, can be cut from the body once the light is found.

Catherine read this message twice. Then placed it on the table, poured a drink and read it again. As a threat it sucked, though part of her wanted to view it more as an invitation. Catherine checked each room, even though her gut told her there was no one there. She stood on the balcony and breathed in quiet lungfuls of warm night air, the ambiguous clue in her hand. The night was beautiful now she was no longer cold. A gentle breeze lilted softly from the west and the gibbous moon glowed a pale and distant cream. It was the sort of night where many things could happen, and would have been happening, if a certain witch hadn't made a certain buttock an itchy embarrassing floral symbol.

No one in their right mind would want to sleep on a night like tonight, but even if it had been minus fifteen and raining meteors, Catherine still would have called Boris.

He sounded as chipper and awake as only hospitality workers can at quarter past twelve on a Thursday. 'Evening Catherine.'

'Hello, dear Boris. I trust I'm not interrupting the greatest moment of your life?'

'It's close. The Vorlons and the Shadows are just about to throw down in a rumble that will make the Galaxy shake shake shake.'

'*Babylon Five*, right?'

'I knew you were the woman of my dreams.'

'And that's where I'm likely to stay in that regard, but something's come up. I need you over here at warp six.'

The tired barman sighed on the other end of the line. 'You know, this is the fourth time I've been interrupted watching this episode.'

'Fourth out of?'

'Probably seven times.'

'Make it warp eight then, Mr Chekov.'

'That was cheap; make sure there's a beer in the fridge.'

Fifteen minutes later, Boris' old white Laser pulled up. He had augmented his usual jeans and jacket with a Boston Celtics cap which Catherine would have to bring up, along with the science fiction, next time Boris went into one of his well-rehearsed diatribes about not finding a girlfriend.

He mock-saluted her on the balcony before ascending the stairs.

Catherine quickly brought Boris up to speed regarding her evening walk with Asher and his fears of Thoth. Boris gave this information careful consideration, imbibing half a beer before he commented.

'He hates people with lisps.'

'What?' Catherine had thought she was ready for any response.

'He names his children Asher and Shiloh and then gives himself the moniker Thoth. It's obvious, right?'

'Only to you dear.'

Boris opened his second beer and passed Catherine a gin. 'I found the car, by the way.'

'The Audi?'

'XRZ 546'

'Where?' Catherine put her gin down on the bench.

Boris took a long sip. 'Just near the church. I guess it was someone at the service.'

'So you followed them and?'

'No, I went home and watched re-runs of *Home and Away*.'

Boris enjoyed Catherine's withering look before stating: 'Marcus Frawley.'

Catherine chuckled. 'Should have guessed, with that pansy arm.'

'Yup. It was remiss of us not to guess it sooner.'

'So you followed, confronted? Talk to me, man.'

'It's a tale of some bravery and intrigue.' He took another long pull of his beer. Catherine counted to fourteen in Japanese, silently. She reminded herself that people who don't mix business and pleasure just don't have interesting enough jobs. Boris found his perch on the kitchen barstool and resumed.

'I followed him back to his work and waited for something to happen. I recalled he had his little rendezvous with Shiloh's people tonight and wanted to check it out. Shiloh came and they went into the building at ten past six. I thought that was going to be the only info I could give you but then I realised I could hear through the window.'

'Were you standing in front of it?'

'No, I was pretending to tie my shoe.'

'For how long?'

'About seventeen minutes.'

Catherine clicked her tongue. 'And you did this even after yesterday's photo and card trick?'

Boris' beer hovered halfway to his mouth, for a second he looked crestfallen.

'There were no pictures tonight, anyway. The skinny of the conversation is that Frawley's trying to sell something back to Shiloh. Something embarrassing, and it's to do with Cassandra. Now Shiloh's shaking him down, and it was Shiloh that got him to throw the exploding soft drink last night.'

'Shiloh?' Catherine whispered the name. Her relationship with the Marr brothers was becoming more complex by the minute.

'Yes, though he was quick to point out he, or "they" had nothing to do with Cassandra's death.'

'They? Asher?'

'No, this is the other thing. Shiloh was talking about a "they" and then mentioned his father. Did Asher mention anything about his Dad?'

'Yes, he did. First he was pointing the finger at Frawley, but I think it was wishful thinking, and an excuse to see me, of course. Then he talked about his father and Shiloh.'

'Does he suspect?'

'I don't think he wants to about Shiloh, but he certainly thinks his father would be capable. Big revelation to me was that Shiloh was in Brunswick on the night of the murder. Which also makes Asher's alibi bull.'

Boris finished his beer with a thoughtful burp. He took another from the fridge.

'How do we find out if Alexander Marr is in Australia?'

'Neal, I guess, would be a good place to start.'

'Too late to call?'

'He needs his beauty sleep.'

'Glad you treat some of your comrades with such deference.'

She planted a fond hand on his shoulder. 'This is what you get for being second-in-command.'

Boris continued his steady drinking. 'Here's a thing. Why get Frawley to try and scare us when Shiloh is actually quite scary?'

'Maybe they don't really want us scared, but they do want him scared.' Catherine's ice was almost melted; it meant she wasn't drinking fast enough.

'You want to call the cops on him? Put him in a nice safe cell?'

'My days of influence with Williams are long gone,' she said, looking out the window. She looked back at Boris quickly. 'Why didn't you tell me this earlier? You could have called me.'

'I always assume you're doing something important and don't hassle you with every detail as it arises. How was I to know you weren't, well, pumping Asher for information?'

'Kindly don't be vulgar dear, you're neither brutish enough to make it authentic nor posh enough for irony.'

'I am the third way in class warfare, it's true'. Boris picked up the mystery letter and took a languid swig. 'I can't imagine that Frawley wrote this. Out of curiosity I looked over some of his copy on the houses he's pushing. Tolstoy he is not. I think there's a different player.'

'Or two. I suspect Shiloh. Frawley would just be the messenger. Plus Shiloh would have a lot more experience writing New Age bollocks.'

'Or it could be Asher just being cute.'

'He is certainly that.'

Boris moved to the couch and lay down. Minty walked in from the balcony and jumped up on his chest. 'But,' he began, as he scratched the cat, 'none of this helps get Melissa out of the frame. You got a flirty message late at night and Frawley's trying to get money out of Shiloh. It all may have nothing to do with Cassandra's death.'

'It's getting us closer. I think we should talk to Frawley again, let him know we know he's being bullied. Maybe we can help him?'

'How?' Boris raised his head, sensing a job he didn't want.

'Maybe he can help us find the father?'

'And in the meantime how do we stop Shiloh strong-arming him?'

'You might just have to put your scary voice on, dear.'

Three hours later Boris awoke to the crunch of breaking glass. He lay on the couch, instinctively knowing he was in no immediate danger. It was from outside in the street, someone's window. He wondered if he cared enough to wake up when he thought of his beloved Ford Laser. Quick as a groggy flash, he was upright and on the balcony. A black car was driving towards Sydney Road. His Laser's driver-side window was smashed. The black car was now turning out of sight. He bet himself a dollar he knew the number plate.

Moments later Catherine joined him on the balcony, wearing a deep red smoking jacket and a satisfied look. 'Four in the morning, and an Audi driver smashes your window. We're doing something right.'

'If he's touched my Tori Amos CDs I may have to kill him.'

Catherine smiled and turned back to her room. 'Get your shoes on, let's go break into Frawley's office.'

Boris rubbed his eyes and looked longingly at the couch. There was an orange pillow on it, which was so comfortable that Boris had dreamed of space travel. 'Are you sure you're not just still drunk?'

Catherine appeared fully clothed in a grey skirt, which matched her top, tan knee-high boots and black tights. 'I don't get drunk Boris, you just get more interesting.'

Up close the damage was baffling. The window had been smashed, but not before someone had written a message across Boris' windshield. 'Leave the mystery to the trinity.' The ink was red; the scrawl was thick, hurried. Even Boris would admit the penmanship was awful. He stared inside at the thick glass that covered the front seat. Boris reached into the back and grabbed a stray T-shirt, using it to shield his hand as he scraped the glass off the driver's seat.

They started the car without trying to wipe the windshield, and as the crisp air rushed in and drove sleepiness from them, Catherine started theorising on what the message on the windshield meant.

'It reads like a heavy metal lyric.'

'Or a fortune cookie, heavily influenced by Christian dogma.'

'Fortune cookies usually make more sense.'

'Have you even had a fortune cookie?'

Catherine looked pensive for a second. 'No. Oh wait, yes once, at a Christmas party.'

'Was it with Chinese food?'

'No, they were by themselves.'

'I think it's part of Uncle Sam's culture that hasn't made its way over here yet.'

'They're sold in the supermarkets. Besides, isn't it Chinese?'

'No.' Boris put on his learned look that he used occasionally when trying to impress people. 'It was invented by a guy called David Jung in LA. In 1918.'

'It's too early for this, Boris,' said Catherine, checking her hair in the mirror.

Sydney Road was deserted aside from an early morning street sweeper, chugging along the footpath. As they passed, Boris looked wistfully at the fluoro-clad gent within. Boris turned the heat up. It was futile against the chill. 'Why do you think we'll find anything here?'

'I'm not sure. It's a gut thing. You saw Frawley here earlier. I think it's Frawley who's trying to scare us to prove some point to Shiloh. Shiloh's scaring him and I wonder if Thoth is scaring Shiloh, too. Also if Frawley's rattled he might be hiding out at work.'

'Is that it?'

'Yes, aside from the other fact I am sure of.'

'Which is?'

'That we don't know where Frawley lives.'

'Good point.'

They parked a few metres from Jewel Real Estate. Boris figured that Frawley knew what his car looked like, so there was no point in being cute at this stage of the game. Through the double glass doors they could see a light in what they both now knew was Frawley's part of the building. The doors were locked.

Boris looked up. 'Alleyway round the back, perhaps we can find a way.'

Catherine's blood was up. 'Let's just smash the doors. He smashed yours.'

Boris smiled. 'We do not sink to the criminal level, Catherine.' He shook a world-weary head and began walking towards the corner.

'Oh, right, of course, let's just go and break in from the back like the truly enlightened?'

Boris looked for a second like he was about to say something, but thought better of it. Arguing with Catherine had always reminded him of playing table tennis against a brick wall.

'Do you see anything?' Four minutes later, Boris was amazingly calm for a man with someone else's foot on his head, though he spoke through gritted teeth. He held Catherine's right tan boot in both of his hands at chest height while her other size seven rested on his noggin. Thankfully some of her weight was taken by her two hands on the wooden fence.

'I see a window that says "break me".'

'Oh good.' He made a guttural noise as Catherine pushed up and over the fence. He barely heard her land, cat-like, on the other side.

There were a few things that Boris considered himself very good at: telling the time without looking for his watch; making crepes from scratch, and getting over fences. In one bound he took the fence, feeling it sway slightly under his bulk and then he dropped, oaf-like, into the small courtyard.

It was only a few square feet of pebbles and stone, punctuated by some forlorn pot plants, and two windows either side of a modest looking door. It seemed to be where the staff of Jewel smoked cigarettes and escaped the stresses of finding people houses they couldn't afford. Catherine was already feeling along one of the windows for weak points. Just as Boris approached the other window she changed tack and found the door open. They shared a look.

'That would have been a lot more impressive if you just started with that.'

'I'd rather be effective than impressive, my dear.'

Inside Jewel was predictably quiet, though half the lights were on. They inched along, Boris wondering why they were inching but assuming there was a good reason for caution. For a second a tall dark shadow loomed near the photocopier, and then was gone.

They found Frawley in his doorway, hands on either side of his doorframe, facing inward at his illuminated desk, the street obscured by the blinds. Catherine and Boris stood there watching him for a long time before Boris broke the tableaux. 'Hey stop the press, realtor found breaking people's car–'

He'd have gone on, but for Frawley's piercing shriek.

His reaction startled them. The man was clearly tense.

He recovered, and took a deep breath. Though he didn't recognise Boris, his mouth twisted into a snarl when his eyes met Catherine's. 'What are you doing here, bitch?'

'Well I had heard that this place did a side trade in martinis. But failing that I'm simply trying to find out who killed Cassandra. I think you might know.'

He stormed towards them. Boris moved slightly in front of Catherine, but Frawley pushed him aside and moved up the hall. Catherine followed.

'Marcus, what worries me is if you're the killer, why start playing school-kid pranks on us? Why the red paint and sparklers?'

Frawley's eyes darted around the room but when he looked at them Boris could see the darkness under each eye. He had slept even less than they had.

His voice was thick as he muttered: 'I could kill you any time. Doing it now might not be such a bad idea, self-defence and everything.'

He took a step towards Boris who didn't move, his face impassive.

'But we could make a citizen's arrest for the assault of my Ford Laser,' Boris replied.

'Don't know what you're talking about.' Frawley was still scanning the walls of the office like he was checking for Easter eggs. Boris watched while Catherine walked behind Frawley.

'Marcus, you've got red paint on your cuff; you're not a master criminal. If you didn't kill Cassandra, you can just help me find who did and this will be over,' she said.

'There's nothing to be over, you cretin. Cassandra was a bitch and that bitch Melissa got her, that's all. Why are you hassling me?'

Catherine stopped following and answered to Frawley's retreating back. 'Because you threw a fireball at us, broke his car, because you're being followed, and because you're scared out of your wits.'

At that, Frawley ran towards Catherine, his eyes wide, and his voice rose in a thick raspy crescendo that sounded like a crow pretending to be a tractor. His arms came at her chest and one hand hit her right shoulder as the other gripped her neck.

Boris moved in sideways, grabbing Frawley and in the process pushing Catherine against a desk. The unyielding wood pounded Catherine's stomach and she exhaled violently against a photo of someone's toddler on the knee of Santa. In the second that followed Catherine registered that she couldn't breathe, that she needed to hiccup, and that Santa wasn't looking at the camera.

As she pushed up from the desk she heard a shrill sound from Frawley and the steady rhythm of breath that Boris fell into whenever he was doing something physical. She turned to find the burly barman soundlessly pinning Frawley to the ground. Catherine fought a second of panic and won, willing her body to relax as her lungs remembered how to inhale again. The pain was not bad, but she would need a minute to make some unladylike noises.

Boris looked up for a second, just a second, to check Catherine, and that was all that it took for Frawley to push a foot against his bearded face and send him staggering. Frawley nimbly returned to his feet and started running.

'I'll kill you,' he yelled as he hurtled toward the front entrance.

Catherine still could not move aside from sucking in air. Boris groaned and made chase, his hand covering his kicked mouth. Frawley made it to the lobby door and momentarily disappeared, then Catherine could see him scrabbling with his keys at the front door past reception. As Boris charged to the lobby door it swung in violently, pushed from the outside as if by a ghost. It collided with the barman's head and shoulder, sending him to the floor. Catherine's eyes darted as the door slammed shut again to the sight of Frawley leaving the building. Followed swiftly by a dark figure hooded, tall and thin. The figure did not look back but moved in the opposite direction of the realtor.

Boris was picking himself up as Catherine came upon him; her hand reaching for his shoulder, a nasty bruise already on his forehead. He blinked twice, groaning slightly. Catherine was aware that every moment she was being nice to him was a moment somebody was getting away. She took her hand off him and stood up. 'Ready?'

He blinked slowly. Catherine knew he was probably thinking about his hammock. 'Yep.'

As they charged out of the building they saw Frawley's Audi tear past in a northerly direction. Frawley was hunched over the wheel. They raced to Boris' Ford, Catherine giving the big man a bump that clearly said, 'I'm driving'. Boris gave no complaint. Catherine slammed her door and had the key turned as Boris entered the passenger side. Her foot hit the accelerator and the car lurched forward.

The force of their speed closed Boris' door for him; he looked up and saw, eight hundred metres ahead, the Audi's tail lights. The adrenaline was cleansing the punch drunk fuzziness of his brain. It was 5.37am according to his dashboard. Other cars were beginning a lazy pilgrimage southbound towards the centre of town, but the northbound lane was still deserted.

As they passed Brunswick Town Hall, Boris noted that the Glenlyon Street traffic lights were thankfully green. Catherine had always described traffic lights as a mere suggestion at the best of times.

'Did you see if he had company in the car?' Catherine asked over the roar of the engine, her eyes not moving from the Audi.

'I didn't see much. Watch that cyclist!' The sound of the Laser's horn squealed into the morning gloom as Catherine turned the wheel in two directions within the space of a second to narrowly avoid a lycraphile. In the side mirror Boris watched his gesticulating frame recede in the distance. The air whipped around them through the broken front window.

As Boris' head slammed back into his seat he held up a pacifying hand and said through a grimace, 'Take it easy, we've got him.'

'You say that now and then later we're at my place waiting for something to happen because – urgh!' The wheels screeched as she avoided totalling a taxi that was attempting to pull into the lane. 'You wanted to play the long game now.'

Both Boris and Catherine's heads leaned towards the horizon for a second as Catherine turned the wheel sharply to re-enter her northwards trajectory. Catherine's manic diatribe continued: 'Well my dear, there are times for the long game, times for manners and times when you just have to go faster than the other–'

The lane change had set off the CD player and Tori Amos' *Live from Venus* had begun. Catherine kept talking but Boris couldn't hear her over the engine and music. He assumed Catherine had said something appropriately ribald.

Boris' eyes fixated on the red light ahead and he felt a lifetime of safety talks with teachers, parents and police officers ring in his ears. He wanted to say something forceful, masculine perhaps, or even charming, but all he did was push back into his seat and say, 'Red, red, red, red!'

A minivan coming from the right entered his peripheral vision. Catherine ignored the light, his voice, the brake, and only just seemed to notice the minivan a second before she deftly swerved to avoid an impact that would have ended them both.

'Yes, Boris, I see it's red, and under other circumstances I would happily just stop and we could chat about knitting or recycled water or whatever takes your fancy but I don't like this guy and I think he knows something.'

Catherine went on in an uncharacteristic display of adrenaline-fuelled chattiness. The speedo was well past one-forty kilometres. As they came up the Brunswick hill they just caught sight of the Audi turning west in to Albion Street.

Catherine continued: 'Oh, going to my place are you? How lovely, I'll put the kettle on.'

Boris made sounds like a constipated toddler as Catherine took the corner seemingly on two wheels.

Catherine's eyes were focused on the black car she was gaining on, still some five hundred metres ahead and going full throttle. It was only the satisfied half smile that gave away how much she enjoyed this. Boris thought of changing the CD, but decided she didn't need any further encouragement. Both she and the Audi had slowed to a speed only fifty kilometres over the limit. Catherine shifted a little in the driver's seat, possibly trying to find more purchase on the accelerator and possibly just squirming due to the broken glass.

'Do you know what you'll do after we catch him?'

'Yeah, I'll ask him who he was so afraid of, and who was the dark stranger who bopped you.'

'I'm guessing it might be the same person.'

'And I'm wondering if he's in the car with him.'

'Let's find out.'

They were gaining; Frawley was barely a hundred metres in front of them.

'There's hope for you yet Boris, and yes he is slowing. Maybe he does want to chat.'

'Maybe he's running out of petrol?'

Catherine checked their fuel gauge, half full and all ready to go. Just like her.

The Audi burst on to Fraser Street. Boris felt he would fall on top of

Catherine as she turned on a pin to take the corner a few seconds later, but somehow their bodies did not touch as her shoulder rose out of the broken window.

If the Audi was trying for an easy escape route it was failing miserably – Fraser Street was adorned with speed humps. The Audi was fifty metres ahead, bouncing like a tinny on choppy seas. Boris mused on how pathetic it looked and would have said it aloud except he bit his tongue as Catherine took the first one.

'Christh,' he attempted blasphemy and then stared daggers at Catherine as she giggled. The CD skipped and Tori started singing about sugar. He braced for the next three speed humps and watched in horror as the black car disappeared from sight, turning east on Hope Street. A large Woolworths truck then lumbered along in the opposite direction. Boris' head swivelled as he looked from the truck's tail lights back to the turning Audi. Catherine pushed the accelerator and they sped past their quarry as the black car took the next side street. Catherine and Boris swore in harmony an instant before they heard the boom of the Audi hitting another car.

Catherine three-point turned the Ford at an impossible speed before they turned into Holloway Road and came into sight of the Audi, now facing towards them having fishtailed around on itself. Catherine turned the wheel slightly right to avoid impact and only then saw shrapnel on the road. Somehow Frawley had turned the car in the opposite direction and thrown what looked like an arm full of ninja stars on to the street beside him. Catherine felt and heard the front right tyre pop and narrowly missed hitting her head on the steering wheel. The car slumped on a forlorn angle and began making underwater sounds. Catherine made a noise like a failing aircraft and Boris swore like a sailor. He turned in his seat and watched the Audi disappear as the Ford bumped to a stop.

Boris jumped from it and charged down the road, jumping over the tyre popping spikes with a grace that few men with a bitten tongue have ever possessed. As he reached Hope Street he saw the Audi moving slowly around a corner some two hundred metres away, Boris could see two people in the car. Too far away to chase.

He turned back and found Catherine out of the car with a serene look on her face, staring at the deflated tyre on the driver's side. The sun was almost up and a few clouds winked pinkishly at them as neighbours began moving towards them, trying to find out if they knew just what that noise had been. As Boris approached, moving his mouth to better soothe his sore tongue, Catherine looked at him fondly.

'Y'know, I've never actually changed a tyre before.'

10

Some people only want to reach nirvana for blog fodder.
~ Asher Marr

Twenty minutes later Catherine was lying in the back of the Laser, hand over her eyes and vaguely enjoying the up and down jolts that were happening around her. There was dappled sunshine slinking into the car, Boris' radio played *I'm Turning Japanese* down low. Tori Amos was now a reminder of what might have been with the CD relegated to its cover. Boris was grunting as he pumped away at the jack beneath the car's chassis.

'Why can't you put the pieces together after you've helped me change the tyre?'

'Oh yes indeed Boris, why not, let's just all do some more menial tasks before doing something important. Let's get that time-waster Da Vinci and berate him for not doing the dishes. Let's bawl out Beethoven for not changing his children's nappies, and while we're at it, let's stone Avicenna for letting the scones burn.'

'No need to get racist.'

Catherine started to rise and thought better of it. 'I'm not being racist. Do you think I was because I mentioned Avicenna and stoning in one sentence?'

'Seemed a little odd to me. You started well and then took a left turn into Middle East executions.'

'Shut up dear, and fix the car. I need gin, breakfast, some sleep and a clue, probably with another gin. Do you have any toothpaste, perchance?'

'In the glove box.'

'Can you see this?' Catherine looked up slightly as she reached for the paste; silently praising the way Boris never cleaned his car.

'No, I can't see right now Catherine; I'm underneath a car trying to jack it up.' As if to illustrate the point, low clunky sounds began from the chassis.

'Oh, don't worry then.' The relief was amazing. If Colgate only knew the power they had.

Minutes later Boris hefted the spare out of the boot, some rags and rusted jumper leads following its path on to the road. 'I think he's probably laughing himself to sleep somewhere.'

'Who?'

'Frawley.'

'I hope so.'

Boris dropped the tyre iron. 'What do you mean you hope so? After what he did to the poor Laser?'

'I suspect we may not see him again.'

'Dead?'

'Yes, those tyre poppers, they seem professional. Not the work of the criminal master mind who broke your window.'

'So he was driving away from us…because?'

'Because the guy in the back seat would kill him if we caught him.'

'Why not let us catch him and then kill us?'

'That's all part of what I'm trying to figure out, Boris.'

Boris turned as red and blue lights flashed rudely at his tired eyes. 'Can you work it out faster? We should get our stories straight.'

Catherine rose to a sitting position after she saw the flashing blues. Out of the squad car came a familiar tall and graceful figure. Thankfully for Catherine, a singular presence.

'Good morning, sir. You seem to have blown a tyre while you smashed up some cars,' said Senior Constable Brittany Houden.

Catherine grinned and lay down again. 'Just give her the facts, Boris.'

Initially cool and business-like in the way of an early morning policewoman, Britt warmed up when she realised that Boris was in the company of her own private milliner.

'Always lovely to find a girl like you in the back seat of a car, Catherine,' she said, leaning on the roof of the Ford.

'You sounded just like Williams then. What are you doing so far from

Broady?' Catherine pulled herself upright. This was fortuitous; she'd meant to call Britt today.

'Temporary trade, I was going to tell you.' Britt's grin became worried as Boris snorted.

'Morning tubby, didn't recognise you, sorry.' She turned back to Catherine. 'Now what the hell have you been up to?'

'Just a flat tyre, Britt. Boris was taking me for a morning spin.'

'I've got a family complaining of their car being smashed into, and here you are not fifty metres away in a wrecked Ford.'

'Don't get excited, we've already spoken with the Al-Faqris and you can clearly see that their car was smashed by a black vehicle. Don't fret, even your superiors can do the maths here,' Catherine said, as she climbed out of the car.

'Morning spin my arse, Catherine. You aren't up at this time unless you haven't been to bed.'

'I went to bed, just not for long.'

Britt looked up the road, seeing for the first time the tyre poppers. 'Christ, what are they?'

'Tyre poppers,' said Boris helpfully. He'd decided Catherine could handle it and had gone back to changing the wheel. 'I've picked up five, must have missed those two, sorry.' He yawned. 'Long night.'

Britt pursed her lips and retrieved the remaining two star-like objects. She gave Catherine a meaningful look. 'I'm getting a new hat every season until I'm forty. Are you close?'

'Close to something. Don't ask. You got anything for me?'

'You're lucky it was me. Now you want something?'

'I'm close, you can get me closer. What do you know?'

'You checked out the bar she was in?'

'It's on my to do list.'

'Leave it. Williams went through it and it's a dead end. Cassandra was drinking with a man who flew back to Sydney immediately afterwards. CCTV at Tullamarine Airport confirms it. He's in the clear.'

'Real estate guy.'

'No. That's why I mention it. Literary agent. Seemed Cassandra Pierce was writing a book.'

'On what?'

'That much I don't know. Plus I've said enough to put me in it with the brass.'

'Ah, but you understand the subtleties of truth, my dearest constable.' Catherine placed a hand on her friend's shoulder. 'You also know I might just find who murdered Cassandra; and Boris' tyres.'

Britt moved back from Catherine's hand, looking around, 'You bloody better.'

Catherine smiled and leaned on the Ford. 'I'll have more chance if you tell me what else you know.'

Britt was suddenly aware of a few residents of the street watching from their front gardens. She made a show of bringing out her notebook and writing Catherine a form of some kind. She spoke so that just Catherine could hear her. 'Short version: no other suspects. The Pierce family's clean. Her colleagues hate her, but nothing there. The boyfriend's alibi checks out. Plus no priors, though his brother and Dad have a rap sheet for grievous bodily harm.'

'Yes, Alexander Marr beat up a girl pretty viciously. Doesn't that warrant some interest?'

'It does. Seems it was some kind of rite gone wrong. Which fits this investigation. But a DIAC search shows he's not in the country.'

'DIAC – Department of Immigration and Citizenship?'

'Yeah, they've given the idea a red light. He could be here under an alias. But it's not where the investigation is turning. Williams is a good copper. The witch did it, the case is building.'

'It's not right. Boris has a lump on his head that couldn't have come from Melissa.'

'I didn't hear that, did I?'

'No. You didn't see the tyre poppers, either. You just found us while investigating a car accident.'

'You know the rules Catherine, as well as me. I bend, but I don't break; even for your hats.'

The radio crackled from Britt's police car.

'Car Twelve, code nine in the alley behind Austral Avenue, Brunswick. Can you converge?'

Britt straightened up. She left without a further word, but her look was heavy. Boris emerged and threw the punctured tyre in the boot as she drove off. Catherine watched her go.

'I hate doing it to her.'

'I think she understands. She's good, and likes helping people more than she likes doing her job.'

'Sleep deprivation makes you quite the philosopher.'

'Someone's got to do the work around here,' he replied.

Catherine and Boris leaned against the car for a minute, watching the sunlight play in the leaves of the gum trees that lined the street. It was a pretty sight, even for tired eyes. Catherine put on her best low officious voice. 'Well, I'll just keep changing a tyre badly and let you talk us out of it, Catherine.'

Boris too, could play the mimic, giving Catherine's clipped tones a workout. 'And I went to private school so I know better than anyone on the planet, and I can just bat my chequebook at a policewoman who knows a good pedigree when she sees one. Then I'm going riding on my pony.'

There was a silence. There was a look.

'Let's never do that again.'

'No, let's not.'

Half an hour later, Catherine sipped coffee on her balcony and listened to Boris plead his way out of the day shift at the Glasgow Palace with a colleague. Given the circumstances Catherine would have suggested that he do the shift, load up on coffee and she join him to while the hours away from the other side of the bar, but when Melissa was staring down jail-time, such pleasures had to be reined in.

'No Jamie, it's not a conspiracy. I wouldn't do this to you on purpose. Look mate I hear you, six hours sleep isn't a long time, but it's double what I've had and I've been in a car accident.' Boris was pacing in small circles, then stopped and stood very straight. 'No, this has nothing to do with Catherine.'

Catherine turned, smiling. It's always nice to be friends with someone so incapable of lying. She was again wearing her smoking kimono and was making more coffee. Boris was craving sleep but she had decided she could wait. She viewed sleep as more a pleasure activity than a necessity.

Someone had been stalking Frawley all night long. Her conversation with Britt had confirmed her suspicion that the someone in question was almost certainly in Alexander Marr's family. One of the trinity that Frawley's scrawled message had referred to: the Father – a dangerous man by all descriptions who seemed to have a past with hurting women. The son – Shiloh, who didn't seem to have any problem hurting people like Marcus Frawley. Then the holy spirit – Asher. Why would he have killed his lover? They were all in the realms of possibility. Fitting the three categories of: tall and thin, strong enough to knock Boris over, and careful enough not to be seen.

Catherine found herself idly scratching her buttock as Boris came in from the balcony. 'Had to swap it. I've got the night shift.'

'I'll try not to organise any shenanigans between five and one then.'

'Ha, three and one. Jamie's such a whinger; students just don't know how to pull an all-nighter.' Boris pulled the top off a nightcap beer and collapsed into the couch he had thought of intermittently for the past three hours.

'What's he studying?'

'English.'

'Makes sense, studying the fashions of interpretation of criticism of Shakespeare in a postmodern dialectic just doesn't inspire the way breaking and entering and a car chase does.'

Boris scratched his beard. 'Fashions of interpreting a Shakespearean diabetic? Are you speaking English?'

'No, but I studied it. It's like a second language to me. Will you call a glazier for your car?'

Boris groaned; a trickle of amber beer ran down the side of his face. 'I'm in no mood.'

'But if you still love your Tori CDs.'

Boris moved off to the phone. Catherine re-entered her lounge room, took the chair opposite the couch and thought about Asher in a leather pirate suit, pulling at the jib on a yacht somewhere in the deep Mediterranean. She could see him drenched in sunshine, his eyes scanning the horizon as if he understood the sea and all her mysteries. He would be less Johnny Depp in those pirate films, more like Johnny Depp before he sold out with that slightly scorched look and a body as taut as galleon rope. He would catch fish for their food and she would bring him tomato juice like Grace Kelly in *High Society* before he would kiss her tenderly on the deck, falling beside her and…

'Do you want to pay by credit card or internet banking?' Boris stood before her, for some reason scratching his left nipple and thus exposing his soft and ample belly. Catherine felt tired, nauseous and further from the Mediterranean than she'd ever been. Boris was a cold shower with a pulse.

'Since when am I bankrolling this?' she snapped irritably.

'Since I was working for you at the time my car was assaulted. C'mon moneybags, no need to get tight.' His hand lowered from his chest and began going into his pants. Boris, when tired, forgot decorum. Catherine, when also tired, struggled to remain fond of him.

Catherine sighed and pulled out her purse. 'I'll pay, you shower. You smell like stale beer and regret.'

'Good idea.' He passed the phone. Catherine spent forty-five seconds giving her credit card details and a further fifty telling the man that no, she wasn't blonde, a Libra or interested.

She threw the phone on to the floor and stared at it. She wondered when Melissa would call for an update. There seemed little to tell, plenty of action, but no proof. Just confirmation that she was in the frame. Boris re-entered with a pink towel on his head. He looked towards the window and smiled his tired smile.

'I love these adventures, I really do. If I ever tell you I'm sick of going out and I'd rather stay home with Gertrude or something, you'll fix it, right?'

'Well, I suppose anyone with the name Gertrude is probably destined to hate me, so yes.' As she spoke she flicked through the pages of the broadsheet. 'Likewise, should I ever say some man is saving me from all this and whisking me away to Rome.'

'Doesn't sound too bad.'

Catherine discarded the paper and leaned back into the beige armchair, curling her fingers around an orange throw rug thoughtfully. 'No, any man who tries to save a woman is not worth it in the long run. Help, assistance, companionship, all fine things to offer, but if a man ever saves you he wants to own you. He probably doesn't even know it, but he'll never forget that you owe him one. It's a bad precedent I want no part in.'

'So before at Jewel when I took the punch instead of you, that was me trying to own you?'

'Oh Boris, that's nothing like what I'm talking about.' Catherine threw him the pillow he liked so much and watched him begin to melt into the couch, Minty crawled on top of him; they made a nice pair.

'You were simply being a gentleman. It would never occur to you to try and own anybody.'

'That's true, I'd rent myself out if I could.' His chest puffed proudly and Minty had to rebalance.

'Don't be vulgar.'

'Not what I meant.'

'It should just never be that I need saving, except perhaps from boredom.'

A few minutes later Boris and Minty were both snoring softly. Catherine quietly made herself another coffee and stood on the balcony, watching children pausing on their walk to school to stare at Boris' poor car. The red writing had been made illegible during the chase, but between that and the broken window it looked like it had passed through a regional conflict to get to Brunswick.

For something to do she reached for her mobile to call Neal, just as her fingers closed around it began ringing. Neal.

'Hello guru of mine. How goes the media wanderings?'

There was a brief pause as Neal exhaled, the closest he ever came to annoyance.

'I'm not always entirely sure you don't just call me guru because of my Brahmin caste.'

'My dear Neal, this is the second time in two hours I have been accused of racism. You and I both know I couldn't be racist because a true connoisseur of the human condition never plays favourites.'

'Hmm,' came the sagacious reply. 'If you're free, why not come round? I would tell you all over the phone, but I do dislike the medium at the best of times and skyping June takes most of my patience for this mode of communication.'

'Do you have information?'

'Enough to reward the burden of the twenty-minute walk.'

'Good, I'm too tired to drive the Vespa. I'll be round in half an hour. But before I come could you do a DIAC search and find out if Alexander Marr is in the country?'

'DIAC search? Haven't you learned some lingo?'

'Life's interesting if you pay attention.'

With that, she left Boris and Minty purring on the couch and set out into the morning.

Catherine knocked on Neal's door and was surprised to wait for over a minute, almost questioning whether her fatigue had caused her to knock on the wrong door, when she heard an apologetic sound and the door clicked open. Neal's face appeared briefly and he smiled.

'Hello,' he said, before his body folded on itself, and he started wheezing with his hands on his knees.

'Are you all right?'

His hand raised one finger above his head while he continued convulsing. To the sleep-deprived eye he looked like a well-dressed wombat giving birth. Catherine waited, trying to stop smiling.

After a minute Neal rose. Beads of sweat shone on his forehead like his brain was leaking diamonds. 'Sorry,' he wheezed, 'June just announced she's coming in January and I am worried I may not allure her as I once did.'

He coughed violently into his fist, 'I thought a few push-ups might get me into shape.'

'How many did you do?'

'Eight.'

Catherine smiled encouragingly. 'It's a small step, but it's a step.'

She stepped nimbly past Neal as he had another fit of wheezing.

After Neal had showered, rested and prayed to Vishnu for a long life he sat in front of his computer screens with a relaxing cup of chamomile. Catherine had never known Neal to be religious, but Neal insisted that in the face of death everyone clutched at a few straws.

'My apologies for making you wait, but I think you'll find it all worth it. I've done some research on the more occult aspects of the murder and have a few ideas. I thought we could, chew the ball around?'

'Nice to know your grasp on English metaphor has moved into ironical.' Catherine didn't look up from her book, *Rituals in Pagan Life*.

Neal smiled, 'I would be happy to converse in Punjabi or Hindi should you have acquired those languages.'

'I'm getting round to it.'

'So in the meantime I will occasionally play the funny Indian guy. It makes me feel like I'm on television.'

'Oh please Neal, this is Melbourne, we're all foreign, we're all home. Some of us have just been here longer.'

'I look forward to your mayoral campaign.'

She put the book down. 'In the meantime, the fingers?'

'You're sure that your friend had nothing to do with this?' Neal gave her a long look as he spoke.

'Yes, I'm sure Mel had nothing to do with it.'

'Good,' he clicked at his keyboard. 'I think you'll enjoy my findings on the question of the fingers then.'

Catherine adjusted herself on her chair, flower forgotten.

'Essentially all the fingers have certain powers in the occult, but the most powerful is the forefinger. It is the forefinger that directs the power of a wand, or replaces the wand should it be broken. The other fingers have powers and meanings: the little finger is the physical body, the ring finger represents the mind, it goes on, and I think becomes less important. If you want to take a witch's, or anyone's power, you cut off their index finger.'

'Which was left alone in this case.'

'Yes, now let me tell you a little about Eostre, the solstice rite that Melissa was taking part in and the police believe may be part of Cassandra's death. It is a time of balance, being a solstice.

'The weighing of positive and negative energy, anything you do will return to you. Should you be placid, peaceful, giving, etc, then this shall return to you over the summer. Should you be selfish, unkind, hurtful, that will be given back to you. Point being, solstice is when Santa Claus is looking, so all the witches you know are almost certainly trying to be nice.'

'Yes, that's what my other research has indicated as well.'

In fact, Catherine had the point two full minutes ago, but had enjoyed the sound of Neal's voice, not quite as much as he did, but enough. He could learn something from Kirsten the magic banker's short bursts of information.

'So no self-respecting witch would do a random kill in this fashion on that night.'

Neal rubbed his hands. 'That's correct. However, further research in Alexander Marr's run-in with the law shows that he might have some form in this area.'

'Go on.'

Neal leaned back in his chair, as if to distance himself from the crimes of thirty years ago.

'It seems that the assault took place during a cleansing rite. A mystic version of an exorcism. It went badly.'

'I see.'

'I couldn't find much more. Though I did find indications that the victim rejoined the movement when the dust settled.'

'Well Neal, if it goes to trial this would be an angle for the defence to use, but I don't think it's going to get her out of suspicion today. What about Alexander Marr's whereabouts and finances?'

'Well dear Catherine, the DIAC search takes time and I'm still recovering from my fitness experience. I'm going to have an early lunch today, butter chicken. I suggest you join me.'

'Tempting, but it's only early.'

'It's eleven-thirty, dear.'

Catherine smiled lazily, 'Time flies for the over-caffeinated.'

'The more theories we come up with the more likely we'll get to the bottom of it.'

'Why not. Let me put this into the mix.' Catherine reached into her handbag and brought out the previous night's personal message.

Neal's brow creased. 'What's this?'

Catherine filled him in. Neal looked worried and then his face split into a Cheshire grin.

'What's your thought?'

'Only that it's good there's more to do. I was enjoying this particular puzzle, and I don't think this murder has anything to do with magic.

'So now I can indulge myself in researching New Age temptations.'

'I love the way you throw yourself into things.'

'This could be a further warning to you and Boris about messing with whomever you're messing.'

'Or it could be romantic.'

Neal waved the parchment. 'This is flowery hash. We just have to wonder if it's also a threat or just run of the mill b-s. The references to the father seem to be coming thick and fast, don't they?'

'Yes, but according to this, there are many fathers.'

Neal rolled his eyes.

'In which case you can just fill me in on what you've learned about the Marr family,' Catherine said.

Neal bowed slightly. 'Yes, that's been rather enlightening in itself.'

Twenty minutes later Neal was fastidiously making noises into a plate of the house special and Catherine was staring into her aloo baigan masala with some intensity. Her forehead was etched with twin lines of concern and her bob bounced slightly as if it were an entity unto itself enjoying the bouquet of spices that wafted lazily around the air.

'How much?'

'Hmm?'

Catherine repeated the question at a louder volume to combat the bustle of the Indian restaurant around them.

'Roughly speaking, taking into account investments, liquid assets and property, the Marrs are worth around four million dollars.' As Neal answered a waiter filled their plastic glasses with the house's most expensive mineral water. She took a sip and looked back at Neal.

'That's a lot of money.'

'Isn't your father's estate about eight times that?'

'I've no idea, I'm sure. And father, bless him, is not in the business of cheap enlightenment.'

'Well, arguably, neither is Alexander Marr. He's in the business of enlightenment which is rarely cheap.'

'How did he do it?'

'There seem to be several factors: his charisma, his luck, a few early believers who seem to have become large donors. Once he got a little break he made it bigger and bigger.'

'And now?'

'Now business is booming, right across the western world people are reading his books, attending seminars that he has written and tuning in to his audio meditations. He was very aggressive in the nineties when it came to diversifying. He moved into calendars, personal seminars, retreats.'

Catherine idly twisted her paper serviette. 'Yet I had never heard of him.'

'You've probably never heard of the world's most famous sumo wrestler, either.'

'I don't know any sumo wrestler's names.'

'Neither do I. And previous to this, my interest in the New Age movement was about on par with my interest in sumo wrestling.' With a rather impressive hand flip Neal neatly popped some naan in some green sauce and then into his mouth in a fraction of a second, without looking greedy.

'I take your point, where does it leave the case?'

'You're the detective, you tell me.'

Catherine leaned back in her chair. 'Money buys goods, it can buy power and it builds prestige. It seems to be a good motive for murder and coercion, which is usually where I get involved. I imagine at some point this case will unravel and it will be about money.'

Catherine wiped her mouth and for a second felt utterly disappointed with humanity.

'Is there anything else?'

'Love, religion and power are the other big three, but in the words of Leonardo, "everything is connected to everything else".'

'I liked it better when he said, "Cowabunga".'

'So that leaves the other reason for killing.'

Neal smiled to himself and continued. 'Do you suspect that love is the motive here?'

'I don't think so,' Catherine said, 'though perhaps.'

'The boyfriend?'

'No, someone else who loved her, or wanted to. Or maybe even someone who wanted to control her. I have a list of leads.' She put her fork down.

'Shall I order some more naan?'

She shook her head, brightening from her momentary misanthropy. 'No, the push-ups you'll have to do for this meal will be enough to keep you going all week.'

'I will not dignify that with an answer. Though since you're buying I will order some extra to take home. I hope it makes you feel better.'

'Mea culpa.'

'Indeed, say three Hail Mary's and buy a fat man some curry.'

'I'm going to need you to keep trying to figure out what – if anything – the cards mean. Last night's message, too.'

Neal looked thoughtfully out the window and chewed the last of his naan.

'You have various possibilities... One: it's the message that the father has returned and will bury the son. Two: that the son – or one of the sons – is burying the girl and using the father as a red herring. Three: that the messages and rites mean nothing and we've wasted a morning, most pleasantly by the way.' Catherine nodded appreciatively. 'And four: that Cassandra was killed by someone we haven't thought of and they are sending a message that we are nowhere near.'

'That last one seems impossible but leaves a rather cold feeling down my spine.'

'We're human Catherine, we come at each circumstance with the baggage of our previous lives.'

'That's profundity enough from you, sir.'

When Catherine's credit card worked some magic on their bill, Neal was quite happily holding some aloo tikki in a brown paper bag to help him decipher the hidden message through the afternoon. As they shuffled through the other patrons towards the sunny day outside, Neal placed a hand on Catherine's arm.

'Also, Catherine?' He was wearing a serious look that Catherine couldn't help but make fun of.

'Neal,' she replied, solemnly.

'Just make sure you don't solve the mystery by experiencing the crime, OK?'

'Cassandra didn't have a Boris, or a warning.'

Catherine stepped out of the restaurant and, for a few happy seconds, felt the wind in her hair and watched Neal nervously cross the moderately busy road with a look of intense concentration. There is little so appealing in life, she mused, as watching someone be so comically safe. He could probably think in four dimensions and crack codes like she cracked jokes, but he was still terrified of trams.

11

Everyone has either a guilty conscience or a poor memory.
~ Kenneth Williams

Catherine's house lay to the northwest, a twenty-minute walk, but she had another destination in mind. The police believed Shiloh Marr had spent the night of the murder at home with his brother. But Asher had told Catherine he had been at an East Brunswick brothel, which Catherine suspected was near the restaurant.

She had never set foot in a brothel, probably the only form of pleasure house she had not frequented. At an individual level she did not judge, but to her mind the oldest profession on earth was just one of the many faces of a million years of gender inequality. Hedonism is wonderful, and yes, the capitalists won the cold war, but some things are sexier when free.

The establishment in question, Coco Lane, was inviting, yet gave nothing away. The doorway was neither gaudy nor hidden. It was, to Catherine's mind, just as full of promise as an alleyway.

Once inside, the room opened to a breezy space filled with paintings of naked women that led to a reception area with a high, white marble, behind which a bespectacled brunette looked up and smiled professionally. 'Welcome. What would you like today?'

What would you like today: what are your most immediate desires, which itches can we scratch? Catherine could see the allure, despite her politics. The job at hand was undeterred, however, and she launched into a spiel. 'I'm looking for a man.'

'Yes we have several for you to choose from. Shall I organise a line-up or would you prefer to look at photos?'

Catherine smiled, pleased that she wasn't blushing. 'I know the one I'm after. He doesn't work here, but he comes here. His name is Shiloh, I was wondering if you'd seen him?'

The brunette smiled. 'I don't know anyone by that name, and we never discuss our customers. I'm sorry.'

'Even if it's a matter of life and death?'

'I'm sorry.'

Catherine stood back, as though she accepted the brush-off. She stood looking at the woman in silence, before saying: 'A young woman was murdered recently. Did you know her fingers were sheared off? They were cut and taken, as if they were morsels of meat. I know this because I found her.'

The brunette swallowed, her right hand fingers caressing their opposing counterparts.

Catherine continued. 'There was so much blood. I found her, and now I'm trying to find who killed her. I know Shiloh, and someone says he was here when it happened. If that's true I can stop looking for him and find who actually killed her. I want to find that person. Can you help me?'

The receptionist looked at her hands, then Catherine. Then she took a breath and her eye caught something behind Catherine's head, a camera. Smiling, the girl's voice quivered as she spoke. 'What night was it?'

'Four nights ago.'

She clicked through some screens on a computer. Saying nothing, not looking at Catherine. She looked in a drawer and appeared to check some pages in a book. Catherine waited while she closed the drawer. She looked at Catherine and spoke quietly. 'You can stop looking for him. He was here from eleven until three. We don't talk about our customers.'

Catherine placed a hand on the reception desk. Not touching her, not giving her help away. 'Thank you.'

The girl was still touching her own fingers. 'Watch him,' she whispered. 'He's a dark one.'

Catherine left quickly, and wished she knew the exact time of death.

The day being as pleasant as it was, she began walking. If not Shiloh, then who? The bulk of the man who had knocked down Boris was powerful. Taller than Asher, she was pleased to remember, it couldn't be him. It was so often the boyfriend, so often love that led people to their end. It was nice to discard the theory. Catherine found herself thinking again about Asher on his imaginary boat, the deck, the sun, the leather. The steady rhythm of the street around her was comforting and she paused for a minute and felt the spring air on her arms and the food in her stomach. She watched the faces of the people in cars, in transit, bored. The living have a duty to enjoy these things, not just on behalf of the dead but for those who live but don't remember (Catherine must have been tired, she always thought like this when she was tired). So engrossed was she in such poetic musing that she almost stepped over the writing. On the pavement in front of her, written in red chalk, was a message innocently proclaiming the two words: "Alexander Marr".

Catherine stopped, blinked twice, and kept looking. The spidery handwriting was just centimetres from her stylish, tan boots. She took a breath, assuming she was being watched. She didn't want anyone to see her panic. She looked slowly around, half expecting to see a black Audi and a thin real estate agent laughing at her. Or a dark figure about to pounce. The street was in a state of bored normality.

Scouring the pathways on both sides of the road, Catherine spied a similar patch of words a hundred metres from her. She crossed the road and trotted towards the script. It was written on black asphalt and said simply "illumination"; the handwriting was the same. Catherine became aware that Cassandra had been murdered less than a kilometre from here. A familiar feeling came over her, a sneer of disappointment mixed with a dash of pity. Someone was trying to scare her in a lame fashion. Again Catherine scanned the scene for an Audi, or Frawley, but saw nothing.

A police patrol car passed slowly, its occupants not looking at her. The park to her right held no one except a woman sitting on a bench wearing black. She was facing away from Catherine and seemed to be drawing on the bench. Catherine studied the figure, feeling relief and a confirmation of her initial disappointment. She bet herself fifty cents that should she move parallel to this woman she would see a distinct and rather impressive side profile.

Alice, the bum-cursing witch.

Catherine had with her a small leather satchel for personal items that are both essential and unflattering in pockets. In an unusual temptation to violence, she began deducing how much damage she could actually do to someone using the bag as an improvised weapon. She decided on two things: firstly, that with a half brick and a decent swing she could probably take the woman's head clean off. Secondly, that such behaviour would not improve the world by any significant means and that getting arrested was not the best way of helping Cassandra, Melissa or anyone. Despite this, Catherine could imagine the satisfying sound the impact would have made. Like a tiny stick of dynamite exploding in a large rockmelon.

As she walked towards Alice, she listened to the witch singing quietly to herself. It could have been an ancient rite from four thousand years ago, passed from master to apprentice, then again, it sounded a lot like Roxette, and so Catherine wasn't sure. What she could be certain of was that Alice had been using red chalk; it was all over her fingers on her left hand.

'Out damn spot, right?'

Alice looked up and her eyes widened just for a second.

'You could work out a pretty sweet deal with Colgate you know.'

'You should not speak with one such as me.' Her voice was dull, as if she were half asleep.

'I'll speak to you, I'll even put on my scary voice if you don't undo whatever you did to my buttocks.'

Alice smiled towards the ground. 'It cannot be undone, but will fade.'

'Neat trick. I guess it's better than cutting my fingers off, though.'

Alice looked at her, squinting with one eye. 'I did not release her soul.'

'She was looking at a wheat sheaf. Seems like a pretty good case for suspecting a mad witch.' Catherine couldn't believe the irony of what she was saying.

Alice snarled and moved aggressively towards Catherine, whose self-defence training kicked in as she sidestepped and countered with an open palm to Alice's chest.

She didn't even go half strength, but it was enough to easily push her back on to the bench. There was nothing to the witch, she was skinny as a rake. There was no way she had been able to overpower Cassandra.

Alice breathed heavily and looked down. 'Don't speak to me, there is nothing you will get.'

Catherine knelt beside her. 'Then why are you trying to get my attention?'

'The father has returned.'

'How do you know this?' Catherine watched Alice intently.

'The signs are there.'

Catherine's hopes drooped. Divining evidence was not going to help Melissa any time soon.

'What signs? Ear of newt being dropped from Saturn? Or perhaps just a single raven, facing west as it defecates on a parked Camry?'

'There are signs, girl. You may not see them, but there are signs. The father has come and will take us all.' Alice's face shook in a slow rhythm. It was just as irritating as the shrill pantomime voice.

'Alice.' Catherine was insistent; there was no reaction from the witch to Catherine knowing her name. She just kept staring down, at either the ground or another dimension or an imaginary friend who was buried four feet below the park. Catherine could have believed all three.

Catherine moved to try and break her eye contact with whatever it was she was looking at.

'Alice, have you seen Alexander Marr?'

'If I had, you would not be speaking to me girl, but a corpse. The father is terrible. He has killed before.'

'Who has he killed?'

'The mother.'

'Asher's, Shiloh's?'

'The mother died, and another almost. You should fear, silly girl.'

'How do you know all this?'

A small patch of saliva had gathered next to the left side of Alice's mouth. 'The signs are there, you should learn to read.' She paused. 'The signs. Especially those that push in a time of balance, which we are leaving now.'

'Do you mean the equinox?'

Alice looked at her, troubled. 'The father has been driven mad by the son.'

'Which son?'

'All fathers are driven mad by their sons.' Alice smiled like she had made a joke.

Catherine stood up again. It was like talking to a mystic fool. 'So now you think that Alexander Marr killed Cassandra. Yet you were hell bent that Melissa did it. What's changed?'

'She is no murderer, but she is unworthy of the power she wields.'

'So you have no problem with her being framed for murder because you don't like her.'

'She will be burned by flowers.'

'Of course she bloody will. Do you have anything else to add, or should I just keep my eyes peeled for some chalk clues? Maybe an esoteric game of hopscotch pointing me in the right direction?'

'Find the son and find the father.'

Alice's hands moved too fast with the chalk in it, spilling her black flannel bag on to the ground. Catherine picked it up, some pills in an orange plastic bottle fell out. Alice barely moved.

'You should go home, Alice.'

'Everywhere is home, nowhere is home. Alone is home.'

'Don't take too many pills.'

With that Catherine left her. Somehow she felt so sorry for the woman but did not want to give her magic credence, and she had confirmed that the curse was temporary. Toothpaste was working its own magic still. On a whim, Catherine returned to the murder scene.

The alleyway seemed painfully normal. Cassandra's blood was gone; a small stretch of police tape was still connected to the fence on one side of where the body was found. Days later and Cassandra's fingers had still not been found.

Catherine walked slowly up and down the alleys that met at a T-junction. She knew the forensics people would have done this, but she trusted no one as much as she trusted her own eyes. Today they didn't show her much, just rubbish and dead leaves moving slowly in the wind.

It was time to check in on Melissa. Even without concrete progress she deserved an update and she was just around the corner. Catherine walked to her street and was fifty metres away when she saw Melissa walk out of her house.

Flanked by two men. One of them was Williams. Catherine ran to them. As she came near Melissa was being guided down into a police car. Her face was ashen. She saw Catherine through the car windows, gave a small smile. Catherine was rooted to the spot. Williams, in the passenger seat, raised his eyebrows slightly at her as the car's engine started. Catherine looked back at Melissa and mouthed the words, 'I'll get you out'. Melissa shook her head as the car pulled away.

Catherine sat down on the fence and put her face in her hands. Just for a minute. With her eyes closed she could hear the traffic of Lygon Street, the wind in the trees. Anonymous sounds, normal sounds. The world would go on if Melissa were put away, if she were found guilty the world would move on. Catherine had to move fast if she was going to stop that from happening.

Five minutes later Catherine checked Melissa's back fence and found nothing out of the ordinary. Missing Boris, she counted to three and nimbly pushed herself over the fence.

The back yard was as she remembered, a well-tended garden surrounding a small concrete expanse, littered with pot plants and dominated by the Hills Hoist washing line. It was unremarkable, despite the many rites Melissa had performed here. It was the scene of many cups of tea and – in Catherine's case – glasses of wine.

Catherine made a sweep of the garden but found nothing more mysterious than a discarded sock. She moved on to the house. The back door was picked easily and Catherine found herself in Melissa's kitchen. Idly, she wondered who would look after Magus, Melissa's cat. Probably one of her disciples would pitch in.

Catherine moved from room to room, soft eyes, not sure what she was looking for but knowing she would know when she found it. Melissa was something of a hoarder, and the police had gone through the place too. It was like a gothic junk shop. She flicked through a book on rites, looking up wheat sheafs only to find a reiteration of Kirsten's words, a prayer for a bountiful harvest and balance within the seasons.

She found what she was looking for on the mantelpiece: a photo of herself and Melissa, arms around each other taken years earlier in that house. It was obviously pre-sobriety for Mel, as they both held what looked to be gins in their hands.

Melissa was looking off-camera and her drink-free hand curled in a pose of magic – in those days Melissa had been able to make fun of herself – Catherine was laughing at her.

Behind them was the shield with the twin pearl knives. Two knives. Now only sporting one, the other no doubt bagged in an evidence room at St Kilda Road police station, or being once again picked apart by the lab of the homicide squad.

Vivaldi chirped from her phone. Private number.

'This is Catherine.'

'Catherine, it's Britt. What are you up to?'

Catherine suddenly felt ill. 'I've just seen an innocent woman put in a police car.'

'Clues?'

'Just that the murder weapon has a twin and I have proof of that.'

'You could tell me what else I don't know about this case.'

Catherine's look was vague, but her voice remained steady. 'I was just thinking about that: the exact time of death; where the weapon is; where Cassandra's fingers are; who slit her throat?'

'Tell me where you were this morning.' Britt's voice was tight.

'Near as I can remember I was in a broken-down car discussing issues of the day with a beautiful policewoman.'

'C'mon, you weren't joyriding. I'm going to ask you a question, and because it's me asking you're going to play me straight, right?'

'What is it?'

'Did your breakdown this morning have anything to do with a man called Marcus Frawley?'

Catherine only knew she'd been pacing when she stopped.

'Yes.'

'You were chasing him?'

'Yes.'

'Same as the last question, did you catch him?'

'No.'

Britt breathed out on the other end of the line. 'He seems to have died not far from where I was speaking to you, this morning.'

'Oh, dear, we were trying to help him.'

'Help him with what?'

'If I knew that I wouldn't be away from my workshop when I have forty hats to make.'

'Catherine, his eyes had been ripped out. When this hits you'll need to come forward and tell Williams everything.'

Catherine's stomach flipped. No one deserved that. She remembered words in the note found last night: '*Only the boldest take this way, for it is filled with a beauty that will take your eyes and a sensory experience beyond the physical.*'

Catherine pushed the quaver out of her voice. 'I'll not put you in any danger, Britt. Why move on Melissa now?'

'I'm not sure. A second death could have had something to do with it.'

'That's just bloody stupid.'

'Don't yell at me,' Britt replied, 'I'm not working the case and I called you, remember.'

She adjusted the volume of her voice. 'I'm not shouting, Britt. Williams has arrested the wrong person and I think the killer will strike again.'

'You remember the address?'

'Heard it on the radio this morning,' Catherine said. 'Thought I recognised that code on your radio.'

Catherine rang off, counted to ten, then dialled Boris.

'Hello, why are you calling from your room?' Boris' voice was thick and blissful.

'Not all of us can sleep the day away Boris, wakey wakey.'

'Something's wrong.'

'Why do you say that?'

'Your words are cheerful, but you've got that fire and brimstone undertone. Don't do it, it's scary.' He paused. Catherine could imagine him blinking his eyes a few times as he often did when tired. 'OK, I'm ready. Go.'

'Neal's pointed out good news: we're right. And bad news: we've got no proof. Alice the witch is talking crap and playing with chalk and we've got another body on our hands.' Catherine began to feel better already, a problem shared and all that.

There was a long pause. 'Right. Whose body? I'm sitting down.'

'Frawley. His eyes were ripped out. And Melissa has been arrested. I saw them put her in a car. We need to fix this, Boris.'

Boris swore quietly. 'You on your way home?'

'I'm walking up Blyth Street, want to pick me up?'

'Sure, I can test drive the car's new window.'

12

It is hard to climb to the moon using only your hands.
~ Alexander Marr

'The car hasn't lost any of it *je ne sais quoi* for all its trials.'

'No, it's a trooper.' Boris took his left hand off the steering wheel to rub the dashboard affectionately. 'You're all right aren't you, honey?'

'Boris, one of these days we'll list the reasons why you struggle to find a girlfriend.'

Boris rolled his eyes. 'Gracious me, is it that time of the season already?'

'Well, if you are interested in coupling we need to iron out some of the eccentricities that shield women from seeing your true value.'

'And the fact that my ex said I was too close with you?'

'You don't want such jealous women in your life Boris; they are vexations to the spirit. They'll sap all of your energy.'

Boris slowed the car and muttered something low under his breath.

'So what are we looking for?'

'Anywhere that looks like a murder scene.'

'This is Austral Avenue.' The street was wide, inviting, normal.

'Britt said it was clean, but we should be able to see something.'

'Let's hope so.'

They parked the car and walked in the bright sunshine towards the bluestones of the neighbouring alley. The suburb was full of such walkways between streets, used in bygone times for the emptying of toilet pans. The first they walked down held nothing unusual except an intriguing piece of graffiti of a Pacman-like creature drawn above the words "I am a naughty cheesecake".

They crossed back over Austral Avenue and immediately found what they were looking for. Invisible from the street, one hundred metres from the T-junction, there were remnants of police tape and the ground had a well-trodden look. Catherine had half-expected a guard of some kind, even with Britt's guarantee.

'We could still be being watched Boris, if nothing else by people in the community keen to know why someone used their alley to kill someone.'

'I'm wearing my innocent face, Catherine.'

'Good. I'm sure that without it they could lock us both up for murder.'

'Great, in prison I could stop drinking and write that novel.'

'I won't let you go to prison.'

'Great, now I can keep drinking and write that novel.' Boris gave a fist pump and kept walking.

They didn't cross the police tape at first, giving respect to the work of the law. They moved meticulously around each side of the alley. Eyes searching, stepping in time to a slow beat that was inaudible. Boris knelt at the sight of something sharp and grunted at Catherine, who looked and shook her head.

Five minutes after they began, Catherine moved into the taped-off crime scene. There was little to see. She wondered why the tape was still up when the forensics team would have already done their work. Whatever end Frawley had met, he had lost a lot of blood. It had spilled in a large patch near the fence of a house and spatter marks were still visible on the opposite fence.

'It looks familiar,' said Catherine.

Boris looked up the alley. 'All too.'

While Catherine stared and put the scene to memory, Boris walked the length of the alley. The wind blew softly across him and he breathed deeply. More than Catherine, he felt death, just for the simple fact that he loved life. It seemed to him everyone did at some level, for him it was just closer to the surface. He didn't mind about prestige, or power. Money meant less and less, especially since having Catherine around with her unlimited cash, but he loved life. He loved food and coffee and beer and smiles and flatulence and his niece. All this was gone for Frawley, never to return. Boris felt it, and liked that he felt it.

'Catherine?'

A minute later she stood beside him. The graffiti looked like it had been there a long time, certainly not done in the last few hours. It was long, about two metres in length, written in capitalised, brown paint. It was a message, clear as blood on a wall, stating: *You will never find "The Way".*

'Well, isn't that interesting?'

'I'm not so sure this has much to do with anything other than creeping us out.'

'That's uncharacteristically self-centred of you, Boris.'

'It looks like this was set up a while ago. That paint isn't fresh.'

'No, but it's recent.'

'How do you know?'

Catherine indicated where the message overlapped another about AC/DC. 'See this? This was done two weeks ago. The message from the killer is more recent than that.'

'How do you know it was two weeks ago?'

'Some bloke asked me to the concert. I said no.'

'Not a fan?'

'The music's fine, I just don't like a stadium show. They're about as personal as tax office correspondence.'

'So is it about us?'

Boris waited for a response, but Catherine was staring at something behind him. He turned, but nothing was there but the opposite wall covered with more graffiti. Boris looked for the clue. Apparently the refugees needed to be freed, someone called Sharlene was a bitch, and a band called Krang sucked. That's all there was, aside from a badly drawn picture of what looked like a man crossed with an Ibis. He turned back to Catherine and held up his hands. 'What?'

'The Egyptian god Thoth was portrayed as a man with the head of an ibis.'

'Somebody's left a calling card?'

Catherine swallowed.

Boris pointed at the first message. 'Strange how they even put "The Way" in quote marks.'

'I guess if one goes to the trouble of killing two real estate agents then a bit of grammar is a walk in the park.'

Boris scratched an ear. 'So my not knowing what a semicolon does is further proof of my upstanding demeanour?'

'Most of your demeanour involves food, beer, sleep and being nice to people. You're a poster child for sloth being struck from the list of deadly sins.'

'I like to think I'm doing my bit for gluttony, too.' He stretched his arms upwards, his soft belly showing from under the frayed hem of his green T-shirt.

'Hmm.'

They moved from the writing on the wall. Nothing else had emerged as interesting or relevant to the case, it was just a sleepy alley, full of promise and a dead man's DNA. Without speaking further they walked to the car.

Boris looked at his watch, 'It's two fifteen. I'm starting in forty-five, I'm gonna get to my place and shower. What's your plan?'

'I'm going to get Neal to do some cyber sniffing on The Way and I'm going to find Asher, unless he's been arrested. See what he has to say about the family business.'

'What do you think about Frawley?'

Catherine sighed. 'That John Lennon was right.'

'Strange days indeed?'

'Most peculiar, Mama.'

Catherine stood at her kitchen bench, shaking slightly. She was glad she was alone. Beneath her, Minty curled slowly around her leg. Catherine put the kettle on. She needed to talk with Asher, or Shiloh, or if he was in the country, Thoth. If The Way was behind the killings, they had become a trinity of suspects in her mind. The dark figure in the real estate office had seemed too big for Asher, too fleet to be Thoth. Shiloh seemed unstable, but was that enough to see him slit two throats within days of one another?

She sipped her tea and rang Neal.

'Hello Catherine, how's the indigestion?'

'I'm fine, Neal.'

'I'm suffering, somewhat. I suspect it's my fitness regime. I did four more push-ups, you know.'

'You're an inspiration to us all.' As she spoke she caught sight of her own lithe figure in the mirror and wondered what she would do if her lightning quick metabolism ever failed her.

'Now I assume you want me to drop everything and look something up for you.'

'That's right. Our realtor friend Marcus Frawley has been murdered.

There was a message at the crime scene – "you will never find The Way". I was wondering if you could do some digging. Did you find out if Marr is back in the country?'

Neal cleared his throat. 'A man with the same birth date called Alex Marling came back a month ago from Thailand, and two men of similar ages called Arnold Marr and Anthony Marr in the past week.'

Catherine wrote it down on a pad. 'That could mean something. See if you can find a match on any of those men.'

'Such work is good for my biceps.'

'June is a lucky girl.'

Hanging up, Catherine decided to cut to the major interest of the day. She called the number Asher had given her the night before, but it went to message bank. She toyed with the idea of a flirty message, but hung up.

She sat on her couch and mused that all women were attracted to a mysterious man. She decided it was likely based on the assumption that a mysterious man will take a longer time to bore you. Or perhaps it was the idea that a mysterious man would show you something intriguing in a world that so often seemed dull. Even to Catherine, who prided herself on her *joie de vivre*, it so often seemed like humanity was a series of water-based organisms distracting themselves with millinery fashions, stocks, elections and Chinese checkers. Filling in the time before they expired and the universe moved on to the next big thing.

Daydreams about whether the universe when photographed from a certain angle would actually look like a Chinese checker board were pleasant distractions from her fatigue. The stars in her mind's eye began to meld with the smiling face of Asher, the eyes of a dead girl and a pair of chalk-covered hands.

Vivaldi's *Four Seasons*, the *Hotel California* of the classical world, chirped at her and woke her up. The clock showed forty-five minutes had elapsed since she had last made a call.

Catherine's phone again chirped Vivaldi. She blinked away sleep for good. Thankfully it was Neal.

'Namaste, Nealamber.'

'And peace be with you too, Ms Kint.'

'What news?'

'Secret societies should get more original if they are going to stick out from the crowd.'

'The way leads you to several paths?'

'It certainly wasn't a googlewhack, no. There seems to be about four hundred different movements called The Way, plus all the connections to Taoism, which I suppose is also a movement, and also Opus Dei, a movement again. There's also a movie, four songs and a play of the same name. One of the songs is a symphony, which has four movements.'

As Neal talked, Catherine found herself, as was her habit, lying on the couch with her feet pointed towards the ceiling. She didn't know why she found her feet so comforting, or the reversal of gravity so irresistible, but she did. After a full minute in this pose she interrupted the serene computer man. 'I can't help but think you wouldn't be so obviously illustrating your hard work if you hadn't found something helpful?'

'You know me well. Here's the news. The Shining Way was founded by none other than Alexander Marr in 1968. It is the spiritual movement behind the giant company. It all seems innocuous enough. Worship of the stars and planets, discussion of Zeus' prevailing influence on matters of earth and space.'

'That Zeus, he just doesn't go out of fashion does he?' Catherine wondered if there was millinery in Ancient Greece.

'I find the idea of a playboy god quite believable.'

'That's because you love to anthropomorphise the gods.'

'I'm only human, now stop interrupting, I'm getting to the good bit. There's been surprisingly little involvement in Australia, especially over the past two decades. A meeting here or there but really the action seems to be mostly in South-East Asia among western expats. However, there was one woman who wrote about troubling experiences in the organisation fifteen years ago. That was back when blogging was rare, but chat rooms were frequent. She wrote about being coerced into sexual relations, having her money taken and brainwashing.'

'And you found that?'

'I was hoping you'd be impressed.'

'Hard not to be impressed, dear. Does she mention who did it?'

'She mentions no names, and there's no discussion on whether this happened in Australia or overseas.'

'What's her name?'

'Her real name is Alison Paulzen, but she goes by the name Alice.'

Catherine's feet came back down the ground as she felt a tingle of excitement.

'Did you see any photos of this woman?'

'Yes indeed, there's a photo on her profile.'

'What does she look like?'

'She's not my type Catherine, I mean she seems nice enough, but I don't know, a hard life by the looks.'

'And?' Catherine began smiling.

'And then there's the nose.'

'The nose.'

'Yes, I think it must be good for smelling coffee in the morning, quite…ample.'

'I spoke with her just two hours ago. She discussed a dark father returning. Seemed stoned out of her mind. Though compared to Marcus Frawley she's doing fine.'

'Yes I read more about that online. Terrible business. In other news I've checked out possible Thoths who have come back to Oz. Arnold Marr is a dental equipment salesmen with a large beer gut. Alex Marling is unemployed and lives in Tasmania. Anthony Marr appears to have no traces I can find through any of my searches. I have to call this one inconclusive.'

'There are bodies piling up and a friend locked up, if you need evidence of how much I need you.'

'I need no such ego puffing. Now, don't hang up yet. In Alice's posting there were a few unsavoury warnings about The Way. Nothing I would usually pay credence to. People chatter about ex-members going missing, without trace. Threats that those who try to expose The Way will be erased in bloody fashion. Usual stuff for the web, but you are dealing with a murderer.'

'I'm practising my high kicks as we speak.'

'And I will cut down my fitness regime to better service your enquiries.'

As she hung up the phone Catherine was given the choice of waiting for something to happen or making it occur. She had decided long ago in life that she was not a waiter, in any sense of the word. She also felt this morning's mix of coffee-based jitters and all-nighter-based exhaustion had been banished by her impromptu snooze. Having reapplied some make-up she took herself outside and headed for The Shining Way. She had a shopping list of questions. The meaning of life she could wait to discover, the meaning of two deaths, she could not.

The shop was open. Catherine couldn't quite believe that the Marr brothers would work so soon after Cassandra's funeral, but if it was indeed a profitable industry then it made sense that they could afford a shop assistant. There was certainly no sign of Asher or Shiloh amongst the colourful clothes, incense and crystals. The back wall was dominated by the larger-than-life picture of a middle-aged man with impossibly impressive pectorals. Catherine recognised him from the newspaper article she had seen. He was long and thin, with a well-receded hairline and a halo of wispy white hair. A round face with proud features and thick eyebrows. His body, which was only partially covered by a robe made popular by Asian monks, seemed two decades younger than his face. 'The way is manifest within you' was written in English and Hindi beside him. Catherine stared at him.

Alexander Marr, she decided, was quite simply the most evil looking man she had ever seen in her life.

The woman behind the counter managed to look serene and paranoid at the same time. Her dreadlocks and henna tattoos spoke of a lifestyle choice of self-acceptance, but her face was that of a stressed librarian. Perhaps, like Catherine, her road to inner peace was side-tracked by an itching buttock.

'I'm looking for Asher Marr.'

'Um, I'll see if he's here if you'd like?'

Catherine decided the poor woman was likely distracted by the impending curse, and so forgave her this idiocy. For a moment she considered telling her about toothpaste, then decided against it. If she hadn't been cursed it would seem strange.

The woman disappeared behind a curtain of beads that when still showed a portrait of the Hindu god Ganesh smoking a bong. The elephant god was depicted as neon pink and seemed to be laughing, though out of his one visible eye a teardrop fell. Within the teardrop a small flower hung inexplicably in its moisture. Even in a week like this, it was an odd thing to behold.

As she waited, she thought about the faces of every murderer she had ever looked at. She had never been able to pick them apart from other humans. She suspected no one could. You can look at anger; you can look at a face that is used to being angry, even cruel. This does not mean you can see a murderer. Catherine touched her own lips and thought about Asher kissing them last night. She thought about all she wanted and all that would be ruined if he were indeed a murderer. If he had come into her life a week earlier, on one of those weeks where she was just Catherine, milliner and lover of life, it could have been a very good week indeed.

She thought of Melissa in a cell, she thought of Cassandra in an alley and imagined Frawley's disfigured face. She decided to stop thinking about what she wanted.

After a few minutes the assistant returned. She said nothing and didn't look Catherine in the eye but moved to the left and sat on a stool near the cash register that was covered in peacock feathers. Catherine was about to speak when the Ganesh beads shimmered and Asher emerged. He wore a loose blue shirt and Thai fisherman's pants. Catherine again mused on his ability to wear the most stupid clothing and make it look dignified. Clothing aside, he looked pale and his forehead was covered in a light sheen of sweat.

'You look beautiful,' he said, smiling at her.

'Thank you, you look tired.'

He smiled at that and gestured towards the door. Catherine walked onto the street and he followed.

'I have a small monkey wreaking havoc behind my eyes.' As he spoke he touched his temple lightly, rubbing a hand slowly down his face.

'Tell me about The Way.'

'The way to what? Shoot the monkey?' He paused and Catherine turned, annoyed.

'Asher, stop being a comic and tell me about "The Way" – the movement – your father's movement. The one I suspect is involved with two deaths.'

He showed no irritation, no fear. He licked his lips and grimaced and said: 'It's the name of the group that father started, not my father's movement.' He grinned, painfully. 'Are you looking for some meaning in the world Catherine?' He began to shake. His eyes widened and he turned to vomit a watery stream into the gutter. He stood hunched over the road, shaking for a full minute.

Catherine rubbed his back and felt it was muscular, strong, and a little damp. He was in a bad way. She could smell the bile. She judged it wasn't the first time he'd done that today.

He turned back to her, wiping his mouth with a black handkerchief. 'I'm so sorry,' he breathed heavily.

She took her hand off his back. 'You're the second person in three days to do that next to me. Is my perfume too much?'

'No,' he smiled weakly, 'big night.'

Catherine wondered what a big night meant to him, if it meant booze or blood. He was already in confession mode.

'After I saw you I drank until God knows when. Funny thing about a lover dying, it gives you the right to drink as if tomorrow won't come. Then it does, and it's terrible. She's still dead and now I'm useless.'

His dark eyes were ringed, she saw, by the dark of a drunken night. The sheen of sweat was making his face catch the vivid sunlight. It was the most welcome thing Catherine had ever seen. She knew about hangovers – her own tolerance and lust for life meant she seemed to miss them, but she'd seen a few. She knew what created them, that careless flick of a heel towards the limits of the flesh. Justifying the moment's lust by the quest to outshine the sun and stars. It was occasionally beautiful and regularly grotesque. The wonderful part to Catherine was that Asher, in such a state, had no chance of bashing Boris, outdriving Catherine or, most importantly, killing Frawley. For the second time that week Catherine wanted to skip.

'You're not very accustomed to drinking are you?' she asked cheerfully.

'Not like some,' he said petulantly.

Catherine blinked slowly, but hardly meant it – his churlishness could do nothing to spoil her delight. Asher's breathing finally became regular and his manners returned.

'I'm sorry Catherine. I feel terrible.' Unthinking, he took a red mobile phone out of his pocket and frowned at it. Then he looked back at Catherine and smiled weakly.

Catherine felt like celebrating, or at least mixing business with pleasure. She marched him east towards Sydney Road.

'Come on, I know what you need. Only thing for it.'

'Let me guess, a clue and a drink?' Asher, resigned, followed.

'Only as to who is killing employees of Jewel Real Estate.'

'Right.' He groaned.

In the cafe, a few hipsters looked up from their goats' cheese momentarily before going back to glowering at street press. They took a table not far from the open windows. Catherine made sure that she could see outside but Asher would be looking in. So there would be less to distract him, so she could be his whole focus, what was left of it, anyway. Asher approached the bar, Jamaican rum for him and a gin and tonic for her. Catherine was impressed that even though he was so hung over he could barely walk and even though a drink was her idea, he still passed money across the bar before she'd finished ordering. They didn't breed many like him these days. She got straight to the bad news.

'So you heard about Frawley?'

'Yes, the policeman called me. Williams.'

'He told you about arresting Melissa.'

'I guess I should feel relieved that it's coming to an end. He's certain.'

'So am I.'

'About who did?'

'About who didn't – Melissa.'

'Oh.' He sipped his drink.

'Shiloh was with him last night.' Catherine was changing the subject and sipping gin simultaneously.

'Shiloh, with who?'

'Frawley, at his office.' Catherine's voice was even. As if she were telling him something he knew well.

Anger flickered. 'How do you...?' Asher paused, sweat forming again on his forehead. 'You're doing your job, aren't you?'

'Yes.'

There was a pause while they stared at each other. Catherine wouldn't break his silence and began to count his eyelashes. She had learned the trick a long time ago. Usually she needed no tricks, but this was an interesting case, with nice eyelashes.

'He didn't kill him.' Asher was certain.

'But?'

'I knew that Shiloh was with him. Frawley was trying to blackmail my family.'

'Did you tell this to Williams?'

Asher took another sip of rum, winced. 'I didn't. I have no desire to see my brother locked up while investigators check if he murdered Cassandra.'

'So why tell me?'

'I suspect you already had an inkling.'

Catherine sipped her drink and smiled. 'Where was Shiloh last night?'

'He was with me for a while.'

'How are you so sure about your brother now? Last night you weren't.'

Asher's face swung towards the wall and back as he swallowed the question. Despite this his voice was calm. 'No.'

'Did he come home last night?'

'After nine everything's a bit hazy. I'm not even sure how I got home.'

There was another minute of silence as Catherine waited for him to say more, to reveal something. It took some time. Asher was staring into his drink and sweating. A waiter gave them a disapproving look.

'There's more going on here than we know.'

'Go on.'

'My father has taught me to see rhythms in life. What we have here is what in orchestral terms is known as a *sforzando.*' The rum was doing the trick.

'You're changing the subject.'

'Only momentarily. I found that with Cassandra's murder there was a crashing boom of psychic power. Then almost silence, and since you knocked on my door, a growing note of hope.'

Catherine took his hands in hers. 'Will this go on long? My friend's in jail.'

'And Cassandra's dead,' he said quietly. He pulled his hands away from the double fist he'd made and placed them next to hers, his dark eyes fierce and his jaw flexing. 'Catherine, I'm scared. The noise is growing, not just for us, but around us. Frawley is dead and I feel the world is rocking slightly. Can't you feel the rhythm falter?'

'Yes, I suppose. I'm more concerned by the rhythm finishing for Cassandra and Frawley and it being subdued for Melissa for decades.' Catherine didn't mean to sound flippant. 'Asher, tell me exactly and tell me now: what was Frawley doing to the family?'

Asher sagged. 'You're so literal. He was threatening to publish some lies that had been written about Shiloh and me.'

'Was Shiloh worried about this?'

'Everyone worries when lies are being told about them.'

'Was he angry?'

'He was, but not enough to gouge someone's eyes out.'

'Then who? Asher, I was attacked last night.'

He did a double take and his hand gripped hers. 'Who?'

'I don't know. It was a dark figure. I was all right, Boris was with me. I'm certain the person who attacked me and Boris was the man who killed Frawley.'

'How can you know that?'

'Because we were with Frawley.'

His hand let go. 'What?'

'I'm doing a job, Asher.'

He looked at her for a long time, swallowing and sweating as he processed this. His fingers tightened around the glass. His hangover made his attempts to stifle his response more deliberate. He was streets ahead of Boris like that, ahead of most people. She liked that.

'OK.'

'OK what?'

'OK, you saw Frawley last night. I'm guessing you're one of the last to see him. Why haven't you spoken to the police?'

'I have,' she said truthfully.

'Was it Shiloh? Or do you think it was?'

'It was a dark figure, tall. That's all I know.'

'Black?'

'I didn't mean skin colour, I don't even have that, just that they wore a dark blue jacket with a hood.'

'Did you think it was Shiloh?'

'Him or you.'

He took a deep breath and then said: 'I drank at least four rums with Cassandra's father. Then a bottle of wine with some of her school friends, the one whose name was Amber. Then afterwards more rum with a man named Trevor whom I'm not sure even knew Cassandra, but we talked a lot about tarot. How's that to begin your cross-checking? You're having an interesting week, aren't you?'

Catherine finished her gin. 'And I haven't even finished one hat yet.'

She caught the barman's eye. Then back to Asher.

'Hey! Did you go straight to the wake after seeing me last night?'

'No, I believe that first I did something remarkably stupid to make you smile. Did you?'

'The message was from you?'

'Did you like it?'

Catherine quoted: 'Only the boldest take this way, for it is filled with a beauty that will take your eyes and a sensory experience beyond the physical.' Asher paled, as Catherine continued. 'It's strange that you said that just before a man has his eyes ripped out.'

He went even paler. 'No, Catherine. I have nothing to do with Frawley's death. The message didn't mean that.'

'What did it mean?'

'That I like you; too much for decency. But I'm a guru to some and a disciple to others. I need to know that you won't just roll your eyes and read a newspaper every time I so much as talk about meditation. So I wrote down some of the things we talk about.'

'So the line about eyes and beauty?'

'Originally it was my father's.' He drew a circle on the table with his finger. 'Sorry.'

'Points against you for plagiarism. I'm going to ask you again. Is your father in Australia?'

'I don't know.'

Catherine wondered if it were time to follow up with Neal. She changed the topic. 'Also, about me rolling my eyes every time you mention meditation? Do you think I'm so one dimensional?'

Asher's mouth moved up and down a few times.

'No, I'm sure you have several. I just wonder if you're too accustomed to hiding them.'

The second gin came. Catherine took a long cool sip. 'I don't hide. I just don't show everything.'

'Me neither.'

'Was Frawley the first to blackmail Shiloh?'

'First what, realtor?'

'Yes.'

'No, he wasn't.'

'This story he wanted to publish, where had he got the information?'

'I don't know for certain, but I suspect he got it from Cassandra.'

13

There are enough quiet people on earth, they're everywhere.
~ Melissa Zamansky

'So it turns out that Cassandra had this information about The Way the whole time and was planning to write a book about it. Asher says he wasn't fazed by it because he knew she wouldn't destroy them, but Shiloh was furious. Then just a day after Cassandra dies who should contact Shiloh with blackmail but Marcus Frawley?'

'Ooph.'

'Boris, are you OK? You just sounded like a female tennis player.'

'I'm just lugging a keg. Why was she going to write a book, I thought she sold houses?'

'Oh right, well, if you sold houses wouldn't you want to do something more interesting?' Catherine's voice chimed out of the speaker function of Boris' mobile phone as he set up for the night's business at the Glasgow Palace. The breakfast shift he had avoided was done and now the Palace was transforming into its true self, a saloon. He had been doing this so long it was second nature, but still manual labour was something Catherine would never experience for long or understand. He frowned into the beer gas indicator as she continued speaking.

'This gives Shiloh a motive for both killings. But it also gives a motive to Thoth.'

'And Asher.'

'He's off my list. My guts are telling me he didn't do it.'

'Guts? Sure you're not being led off the scent by a more southerly organ?'

There was a pause. Boris knew that she wouldn't like that, but a lackey doesn't have to be a sycophant.

'No Boris, Asher's appeal has not blinded me to his motives. He said he went back to the wake and wrote himself off. You should have seen him. I haven't seen anyone that hungover since you after the Christmas party last year.'

A shiver went through Boris' body as he took a bar stool off the bar and put it in its place.

'Leon told me it was what the Romulans drink.'

'Yes, a successful campaign for Midori if ever I've heard one. I certainly don't think someone that messed up could have orchestrated that car chase a few hours ago. They were professional tyre-puncturing stars; from what I saw today, the best Asher could have done then would have been a snore and possibly some drool.'

'What do you see in this guy?'

'I'm always intrigued by the possibility of tanned, prominent abdominal muscles; a girl is allowed some weakness, Boris.'

Boris muttered into a handful of coasters.

'Pardon?'

'Just saying that we should track down Shiloh as soon as possible.'

'Yes, it does seem to be the bleeding obvious. I just want to try and find out if this Thoth thing has legs. I saw another photo of him. He's tall, but he must be about a million years old by now.'

'What about Alice?'

'Oh, yes. Neal got back to me – she was in The Way!'

Boris could imagine her jumping up and down slightly as she said this. She sounded happy, and slightly left of sober.

'You mean "in The Way" as in the spiritual group which seems to be killing people or in the way of your shopping trolley?'

'Do I need to answer that?'

The stools were in place and Boris was wiping tables. 'It's all very connected; do you think she should be on your list?'

'She's too weak to overpower anybody, plus she's crazy enough but not methodical like our killer.'

Boris blinked twice against the glare from the outside sun. 'I could ask her, she's here.'

'Really?'

'Yep, outside staring at me through the windows. What was she wearing today?'

'Faded jeans, black cotton hoodie. Bit hot for a day like today I should think.'

'Yep, I think it's her, didn't you say she seemed sedated earlier?'

'Aside from the use of chalk I would say she was in a coma.'

'Looks like she's woken up. You weren't kidding about the nose were you? I'll call you later.'

'Boris, if she says anything about flowers, get out of her way.'

Boris closed his eyes and digested this. He decided not to ask. 'Right.'

As he hung up the phone, he saw that Alice was staring through the window, not necessarily at him but at many things, her eyes darting, stopping on points, waiting a second and then darting again. She had eyes, Boris thought, like dying road kill. Her whole body was pressed against a window, as if the pub was drawing her in like a vacuum. Boris could relate to this, but not in such a literal way.

The clock above the coffee machine showed half-past four. There were some customers out in the beer garden, but the inside of the place was empty. The doors were unlocked, but he pushed one open for her.

'Hello.'

She pushed past him. Eyes scanning the room, she walked to the middle of the tables and back towards the bar. Then drifted left and stared for a few seconds at the stag head which adorned the doorway to the beer garden and table tennis. As a stage entrance it was great, she filled the room. When she turned back, Boris was at his station behind the bar. She looked at him for a long time, it seemed. Boris looked back at her, smiling a little.

He had been taught that when a "crazy" came into the bar to give them no attention, just starve them of an audience for long enough so that they moved on to the next distraction. Boris broke this rule as often as he could. He felt a natural sympathy for the lonely. Also a fondness for people who didn't fit into society easily: 'The poor souls,' as his father would say. So he kept a steady gaze with Alice and continued smiling. She eventually broke the silence.

'Is she here?'

'No one's here but me, madam. Would you like a drink?'

'Where is the one who was burned by flowers?'

That sounded familiar, but Boris couldn't place it.

'Not sure who you mean. We have some lovely Tasmanian pilsner on special this week, beautiful bouquet.' He always wondered who he was sending up when he spoke to people like this.

'She's the pretty one, not for long. Drinking all the day. Has the hair.' Alice karate chopped the air near her chin.

'Oh, I know who you mean. No, she's not here.'

'She was burned by flowers.' The witch grinned. Boris considered how best to end the conversation. His experiences with his two-year-old niece taught him that in conversations like this, a tantrum was never far away.

Alice suddenly looked at him squarely. 'Do you seek the father?'

Boris moved to the coffee machine. 'I have all the enlightenment I need, thanks.'

'The father will burn them all. Fear the father.'

Boris paused. If he ended up in yet another six-hour chat with a born again Christian he was going to kill Catherine.

'Do you mean Thoth?'

Alice's face ignited. 'You know him, you will burn!' She ran towards him with arms held wide.

Boris smiled, as he often did when someone was yelling at him. 'I don't know him, but I've heard of him. When did you last see him?'

'Burn.' She had stopped moving, but was just a foot from the bar with her fists about her chest as if she were about to ski the last metre between them.

'Did you call him Thoth or Alexander Marr?'

'Burn.'

'Did you last see him in Australia or Thailand?'

'Burn.' The cries were getting more shrill, but somehow weaker.

'What year was it?' Boris' voice remained calm but direct; you could hear the care in his voice.

Alice made a sound like child who has touched the kettle. Her hands dropped to either side and her body crumpled. She crouched on the ground, quietly sobbing. Boris flicked a switch on the coffee machine and made her a peppermint tea. He took her by the arm and led her to a table, sliding the drink over to her. She looked at him with grey eyes that suddenly didn't seem at all clouded.

'It was ten years ago, in Thailand at the last.' She sipped the tea, spit momentarily linking her and the cup. Boris ignored it. 'I had followed

The Way for years. I was in love with the master – that was what we called him. Even after he had almost broken me while I was still a girl. He had several other women. But it was when he gave me to the other men that I was broken. I have never recovered. I even learned a curse so I would be able to have some revenge. It's not very good though. Half the time I am lost and half the time I am angry. You're a very clever boy to calm me down. I think the father has returned. I have seen it in the cards and the bones.' It was as though she was trying to get it out before she became lost or angry again.

'Did you see him?'

'No, I used the cards and the bones for many years. Even before The Way, though the master was fond of them.'

'Tell me Alice, did you ever know the master's two sons?'

'I knew them, they are still here. One is anger and confusion, one is cold. He has much of the father in him.'

'Which one is that?'

Two men in fluoro vests came in. Ever attentive to duty, Boris gave Alice a "hold that thought" look and got up from the table. He promptly set up two pots and a bowl of peanuts. In the moments he faced away to put their money in the till, Alice left. Boris waited five minutes in case she had gone to the ladies' room, but she had gone. More customers came in; Boris served beers and wondered what it all meant.

He usually did this, the wondering, but today was more focused and the thoughts filled his hours. Alice was broken by The Way and had an axe to grind. Was it possible that she had supplied part of the story to Cassandra? Both the brothers sounded pretty messed up, the way most of Catherine's boyfriends were. Though one sounded worse than the other. If Shiloh had killed Frawley was he now fleeing, possibly to Thailand to be with the father? How much of this should Catherine know? It distracted Boris from the change in the till issues, the drunks, the students, the interminable time it took for Leon to change a keg. He enjoyed the focus and was happy and thankful for his job and his place. Every murder has its silver lining.

After she had hung up from Boris, Catherine committed her second count of breaking and entering in six hours, at flat 12, 28 Mitchell Street, previous residence of Cassandra Pierce. Catherine had walked the length of the street looking for plainclothes police and found no sign. Either they were stretched with the new body or they had given up on this part of the investigation.

As she walked into the doorway, she thought about how a love of hats can make you a better thief. , She had first made a hat when she was about fifteen. When her aunt was battling cancer and she had wanted to help. Having taken some rudimentary lessons from the art department at school she had embarked on something simple and stylish that would cover Heather's bald head.

Catherine had loved the feel of the felt in her hands, as she had moulded, pressed, fought and hewn the material that gave her what had she learned to call the "craftsperson's stillness", where the brain became quiet.

It had become a hobby, and years later, a vocation. Catherine had become adept at the craft, the materials and the accessories. Including hair and hat pins, which had, in turn, shown their other properties in time, such as lock breaking. Sometimes she wondered if she really needed keys.

It had taken the better part of two minutes getting into Cassandra's, and she did not have much time. It was a one-bedroom apartment, rich in colour, with orange and pink the main offenders. Catherine moved first through the living area. Nelson Mandela held a hand above his head in a framed poster above the mantelpiece, just next to the large television. The mantel boasted many photos of Cassandra. Her smile dominated – with Asher at a wedding, her on a ski lift, at the beach with her sister Anna. Catherine moved to the laptop on the coffee table. It was locked, Catherine attempted four times to guess her password, without success. Hat pins were useless against locked computers. Catherine checked the book shelf for files. More than anything, she wanted to see the documents that Frawley was holding over Shiloh. There were several titles such as *The Fifteen Rules of Power* and *The Seven Habits of Highly Effective People*, but no files about The Way.

Catherine searched the bedroom, quickly and quietly. The neighbours presumably would have found out about Cassandra's fate and she did not want them calling 000 to report a looter.

Cassandra was a snappy dresser with a great number of fabulous shoes. Catherine was interested to find very few male clothes, which after a three-year relationship with Asher should be in evidence. Nothing seemed out of place, nothing was suspicious. It was a normal 28-year-old's apartment.

Under the bed she found a ring. It was chunky, not a woman's ring. It seemed like the ring a man would wear on his little finger. She immediately thought of Shiloh's hand when he slammed the door on her three days earlier.

One hour later, Catherine was sitting in a visiting room at the Phyllis Frost Correctional Centre, where Melissa was being held until her trial. For a prison designed to house a maximum of two hundred and sixty, the jail was heaving, with close to three hundred calling the place home. Solitary and the protection wing were taken up mostly with general population prisoners. Melissa, due to the interest in the case, was being held in the protection wing. In the visiting room, the traditionally unadorned walls had a calendar on them mysteriously stuck on April; it showed a picture of the Gold Coast. Catherine wondered if it had been placed there just to increase the already depressing nature of the rooms.

After a ten-minute wait Melissa appeared with a male guard who looked twice at Catherine as if he recognised her. Without saying anything, he watched Melissa enter the door and promptly left.

Melissa sat down and looked at Catherine with raised eyebrows. 'So, jail's depressing. Jesus wept.' She blinked as if something were in her eye, then looked up brightly. 'How's your day?'

Catherine couldn't help but laugh. 'Improving.'

'They haven't said much to me aside from asking me about murder weapons, fingers and now eyes.'

'It's crazy. How's your lawyer.'

'Young. Just wants me to say nothing. It's irritating. The first murder was mad, them thinking I did it. Now they've got me ripping a guy's eyes out.'

'The screws giving you grief?'

'Ha. No, a bit of stuff about witch burning. Nothing original or helpful. At least I can smoke.'

'I'm struggling to think how they justify keeping you here.'

'One of my songs has a line about ripping people's eyes out.'

'That's pretty weak.'

'I was out last night. Just for a walk, then I stayed out till dawn, just walking. Thing is, I did a good job of giving the cops who've been watching me the slip. Wish I hadn't now.'

Melissa's eyes were on the table and her cheeks looked momentarily as drab as the room.

Catherine pressed on. 'Tell me about The Way.'

'The way?'

'Alexander Marr's movement?'

Melissa leaned back in her chair and looked at the Gold Coast calendar.

'Can't tell you much, I didn't ever have much to do with it. I've just heard of him the way you've heard of Madonna.'

'The more I poke into this the more The Way keeps coming up. Right now I have two suspects, both connected.'

'Who?'

'One is Asher Marr's brother Shiloh, the other is Alexander Marr himself.'

'I could believe that.'

'Why do you say that?'

'Marr is known as a cruel man. Powerful. I've heard he's stopped ageing.' Melissa's face was unreadable, but she ran a hand slowly across her left cheek. 'I didn't think he was even in the country. As for Shiloh, I met him a few years ago. At a ritual. He seemed nice in a stuck-up, short fuse kind of way. The same people he got pissed off at also pissed me off, so I guess I liked him. He did mention that his brother was a prick. You met with him?'

'I have.'

'And he's off the list?'

'As of about two hours ago.'

Melissa paused and wrinkled her nose. 'Don't miss anything. Hey, can I give your number out to magazines? I think a few will try and contact you but my lawyer won't let me do media before the trial.'

'I'd rather you didn't, Mel.' Catherine made sure her expression was blank, even though she wanted to slap her friend.

Mel seemed to get it, and looked shamefaced.

'I gave it out to one. Just ignore the call.'

'I just want to get you out of this. Fame can wait, right?'

'Yeah, I just don't want to miss it.'

Catherine wanted to change the subject.

'Boris had his suspicions about Asher, too, and the partner is always the first suspect, but I can't see him doing it. Plus for the second murder he had a good alibi.'

'You checked it?'

'He puked at my feet he was so hungover. Plus I caught a glimpse of the culprit last night, nimble as a cat and strong enough to topple Boris.'

Melissa's eyes lit up.

'Nice to know you're getting into it.'

'I'm in it up to my armpits, so just keep avoiding a shiv in the showers and we'll be right.'

'They're all terrified of my evil eye.'

Catherine took her wrist in her hand. 'I'm working babe, honest. I'll pass on a photo of the shield at your house to your lawyer. It shows two knives.'

Melissa returned the grip, smiling darkly.

'They'd just say I threw one away after I killed her.' She managed a chuckle.

Catherine couldn't quite laugh along. Plus her lily was flaring up.

'Oh, that reminds me. That flower thing that Alice does, you said it was temporary, so did she. How long?'

The guard returned and grunted their time was up. Melissa stood up but paused at the doorway.

'Toothpaste's the thing. It'll stay for about a week; in the meantime just use toothpaste.'

14

Only in defeat do the good stay pure.
~ Shiloh Marr

Once outside in the afternoon sunshine, Catherine felt the fragile exhilaration that only comes from leaving a prison. From the age of seven Catherine had known that one day she would be sent to a brig of some kind. When still at school she found her exuberant nature got her into more trouble than others. With this in mind, she had worked her entire life to build layers of cheer and happiness into the very folds of her brain. So that when that terrible day came, when there would be no friends, no gin, no walks through windy parks and no rock and roll to dance to – she would be ready. Don Walker said: 'They build jails for those who can't build their own.' Catherine had built within her a private escape hatch, which protected her from being scared into obeying the rules.

A yellow cab swerved to pick her up. She sat in the back seat and wondered where to go. With no other options presenting themselves she directed the driver to the Glasgow Palace. Many a lead became obvious after a drink, and she hadn't had one in an hour and a half. It cleared the neural pathways, or something.

Her phone interrupted this course of thought, chirping more Vivaldi at her. If Catherine had been the sort of person who put reminders into their phone, she would put one in about getting Boris to change it to Doctor John.

'This is Catherine.'

A male on the end of the line inhaled noisily and sighed. Catherine's first thought was that Boris had stumbled over another body.

'Catherine, sorry, it's me.'

She recognised Asher's voice. Catherine smiled at the idea that he had become an "It's me". It turned a light on inside her.

'Hello me, why are you sorry?'

'Because I'm going to bother you. Shiloh's missing. Could you come over?'

'Yes, sure. What do you mean missing?'

'Just that. I can't raise him and no one has seen him since this morning. I'm sorry, I just don't know who else to call.'

'Sure, I'll come now.' She rang off. 'Change of destination, please driver.'

Once at the shop of 'enlightenment or whatever' – as Catherine had taken to calling it in her head – she was silently and immediately ushered through the smoking elephant god beads and directed through a stock room. It was the same shop assistant, unhappy to see Catherine. She seemed the kind of hippie who professed to love humanity, while loathing almost every person they meet. Past the stock room was a narrow staircase of varnished dark wood so steep that it almost seemed more like a ladder. Clearly Asher and Shiloh had no friends confined to a wheelchair.

The simple nature of the shop had puzzled Catherine: why did rich men like the brothers Marr live above a shop? Once upstairs her curiosity was sated. It was a case of: if you have it, don't flaunt it. The room's high ceiling was dominated by a huge skylight, which drenched the room in sunlight. Opulent couches of leather and a thick shag rug were placed about the room. Ornate carvings of gargoyles and Egyptian gods were placed stylishly in corners and beside doorways. Three long windows that stretched across the eastern wall showed the rooftops of Brunswick. The skylight bore no cobwebs. Catherine was further impressed. On a clear night it would be beautiful, today it was merely stunning. Catherine, who loved her northern suburbs deeply, was suddenly overcome with a strange feeling of unbelonging. This room didn't fit in Brunswick the way a chandelier wouldn't suit a tractor barn.

Architectural admiration aside, Catherine was also immediately taken by the figure on the leather couch. Asher was topless and obviously distraught.

Catherine's greeting caught in her throat. She had difficulty not lingering on Asher's flawless physique. He had a professional dancer's body, with broad shoulders, prominent pectorals and beautifully defined abdominals. These would usually have dominated Catherine's vision, but Asher looked worse than he had three hours ago. Now he seemed haunted.

'What's happened?'

'Thanks for coming.' He half stood until she sat beside him on the couch. 'Shiloh seems to have gone missing. I wouldn't usually worry, but with everything that has been happening, I'm afraid I've panicked a little. Have you heard anything?'

'From him, no.' This was no time to bring up finding his jewellery under Cassandra's bed, so she continued. 'What's got you so rattled? Just three hours ago you were fine aside from a somewhat brutal hangover. I thought by now you'd be coming good, not falling apart in fraternal concern.'

'Well, I didn't see Shiloh last night, but that could have meant anything. It's just that he had a morning meeting, which I know he usually wouldn't miss in a pink fit. About money. I just got a call from our lawyer and Shiloh can't be contacted; his mobile is going through to message bank.'

'Do you have another number for him?'

'Yes, I have this.' From the bench he picked up the small red phone. 'He has one, too. We only use these phones to call each other when needed. No one else has these numbers. I know it seems a little cute, but sometimes we just need a private talk or occasionally when one of us needs some space from the world, we can leave it all and we can just call to check in on one another.'

'And when you call?'

'It's off. It's supposed to never be off. We have a deal.' Asher looked like he was about to cry. Catherine flipped into business mode.

'I need to know the last time you spoke with him and saw him.'

'I saw him at the wake before I came to see you last night.'

'Did you tell him where you were going?'

'No, he understands that sometimes I have to leave without discussing everything.' He held up the phone. 'He's got my number.'

'Would he have disapproved of you leaving to talk to me?'

'He probably thought I was doing it because you're beautiful and I was sad. And yes, he would have disapproved. But it's not enough for him to go off the grid like this.'

'And what exactly was the meeting this morning?'

'A meeting with our lawyers. Some land we purchased a while ago is about to be sold. Shiloh does a lot of the signing for stuff like that. I let him keep more of the money for it. He likes that.'

'Is Shiloh more interested in money than you?'

'Shiloh is more interested in money than most people on the planet. I also got a call from someone who sounded like my father. The connection was terrible, but I think he might be in Australia, and he didn't sound happy.'

'What did he say?'

'Something about being disappointed and coming to fix it all. Then the line cut out. He called just after you left.'

'OK.' This was getting warmer. Catherine wondered if Asher had some gin. She ignored the idea and pressed on. 'About Shiloh, did you speak with him after he spoke with Frawley last night?'

'No, I just knew he was going. I told him not to worry about it, especially in light of Cassandra's death, but it just made him more determined to tie up all loose ends.'

'Was Cassandra going to betray you?'

He stood up. 'No, probably not, Cassandra just liked to win. She just wanted me to know that because I had money she wasn't my slave.'

'Why would she think that?'

'I don't know, I treated her well, I think. It wasn't always that serious between us. Maybe that was the problem.'

Catherine noted that yes, that kind of thing was usually a problem, but said nothing.

Asher continued: 'She just loved winning. Shiloh was furious when I told him about it. They were close too; he took it as a much greater betrayal.'

'How close is close?' Catherine thought of the ring in her handbag.

He stiffened. 'Just close.'

He sat down again. They stared at each other, neither blinking. Both were saying things without speaking. Catherine wondered if they were having the same conversation.

Eventually Asher turned and stared out the window. 'I know you're just trying to get to the facts. The police were the same without being so intimate about it.'

Catherine did not smile. Some jokes aren't to be laughed at. She sat very still, waiting.

After a while he spoke again. 'When we were boys, Thoth would occasionally take us to the beaches on the bay for a few days. I remember it as three days of running. Thoth was very big on tiring us out, he would make us race and race all day. Around rocks, up dunes. We loved it and were always laughing. But I was always faster. Being the eldest that's not surprising. But you know I didn't realise until many years later how many times in a day I used to beat my brother. So many times Thoth would praise my feet and then grin at Shiloh, just grin at him. Not admonish him for losing. Just a grin and then he would come up with another race that I would beat him at. I wonder now, what that does to a man.'

He looked at her, and his eyes opened and narrowed within a second. It was alluring.

'Do you ever think about dying, Catherine?'

'I believe it's part of the deal, so yes, I'm reconciled to it.'

He looked at his hands, splayed in front of him. 'Does it make you afraid?'

'It depends; I think if I'm conscious of me afterwards I'll miss things – sunlight, gin, music. I don't think that's how it goes.'

'No.'

'I doubt I'll even notice.'

His face was very close to hers. 'Catherine.'

'Yes.'

'You know, right now, I really don't want to die.'

Catherine placed her right palm on his chest. 'I don't think it's on the cards at the moment.'

'I think I might be next.'

Her face was close to his. 'Who are you afraid of?'

Asher lowered his eyes. He took her hand in his. She did not object.

'Would you come with me Catherine? I have money. We could be in the air in an hour.'

Catherine rocked back; her eyes closed. 'Asher.'

'I don't like admitting I'm scared, but there have already been two deaths. And with you I feel so happy.'

He kissed her. She, despite herself, kissed back, gently. His hand rose to caress her face and as their lips broke contact Catherine felt a lifetime of promise in the air. Of travel and passion, shared jokes and minor squabbles. Of shared time. It was a promise that perhaps she wanted but didn't think of. A girl doesn't, if she can help it.

'I can't,' she heard herself say. She was standing up, completely ignoring the pull of her body. 'After this is done.'

Asher stood fast, taking her hand quickly but gently. 'After this is done there will be more death. I may be gone. This could be our only chance.'

Catherine stared into his eyes. They were steady, they didn't look like pleading eyes.

She turned away, walking towards the middle of the room, breaking the spell. 'Melissa didn't kill Cassandra, Asher. I can't leave my friend in prison. Nor can I leave if Boris is in danger.' She turned. 'And you can't leave Shiloh.'

'I don't want to, but what if it's already too late?'

'We don't know that. What if Shiloh has come to harm, too? Where would Shiloh go if he wanted to be alone?'

'I don't know. He's alone a lot.'

He reached for her. But she was out of reach, already moving towards the stairs.

'Catherine, where are you going?'

'I've got an idea. You want to come?'

'No, he might come back here. Please don't go.'

'Why not?'

'I'm afraid for you.'

Catherine squared her shoulders. Then relaxed them. Even if he were right, she would still have to know what happened. She had promised Cassandra's memory, promised Melissa and promised Asher to find out what happened that night. She looked at him.

'Do you know what I find really useful about fear?'

'What?'

'Absolutely nothing.'

He made no sound as she walked down the stairs. As she came to the bottom he called to her. She turned and he threw something to her. Catherine looked at the key in her hand. 'What's this?'

'Just be careful. I'll be waiting for you.' He smiled.

Bravery and common sense were themes that ran through Catherine's mind as she walked to the place where she hoped to find Shiloh – the grounds where she had watched him cry. Around her the air shimmered almost golden in the dying sunshine. She was not the sort to be swayed by a kiss, though there is something magical about the act of pressing a mouth against that of a desired other. Prelude to a dalliance.

It made sense that Shiloh had gone to ground. If he had killed Frawley he could be at the border by now, but if he was not the killer, then Catherine may indeed find him contemplating his navel at the Alex G. Gillon Oval. Possibly doing more martial arts, possibly just getting stoned. Possibly watching the Brunswick Junior Football Club play an evening game.

Catherine made her way to the ground and found it almost deserted. On the far side a few children played on the swings and equipment, watched by a parent. A couple walked a golden retriever and held hands.

Catherine made her way between the seats on the pavilion and thought about rival brothers. It went back to Cain and Abel and probably beyond. Would the first murder have happened if God hadn't shown such ridiculous favouritism? The problem with God being both omnipotent and regularly disappointed was that, under scrutiny, God appeared as something of a drama queen. She filed it under "moves in mysterious ways" and got back to the job.

Catherine sat and watched the football ground. She didn't know what to do next, and so for a minute, she did nothing. She could go back to Asher and comfort him; she could go to the pub and drink until closing time. She could take the news of the phone call to Asher from his father, the DIAC issues and the photo of the murder weapon to Williams, and see if they could put aside old differences and solve the crime.

It was while she sat there that she smelt a change in the air. Someone was smoking marijuana very close to where she was sitting.

She walked down the stairs and circled the pavilion. The doors were locked. She moved around the back and saw no one. The smell was gone, too.

As she was returning to the front of the stands a movement caught her eye. Or not so much movement as the flicker of a light being switched on inside the pavilion.

The lock resisted her pins for three minutes. Catherine was sweating despite the cool as she opened the door. She moved through empty change rooms, checking each shower, finding nothing but a foul smelling towel.

There was a door at the far end. The light was showing from underneath. Catherine inhaled, and the kiffy smokiness was there again. She opened the door. It swung silently.

Shiloh was facing away from her, reclined on a couch looking towards the list of the Brunswick Cricket Clubs century makers since it joined the Sub-District Association in 1909. He was smoking a small joint; the remnants of four others were butted out next to the couch. Aside from the florescent bulbs that Shiloh had turned on minutes before, light came from three high windows, which topped three of the four walls. Through them, Catherine could see eaves of the stadium and trees in the nearby park slowly changing colour as the sun went down.

'Hello, Shiloh.'

He turned, his rat-like face quick with fear before morphing into a stoned, impassive stare. 'Have you seen my brother?'

'Yes, he's worried about you. He said you didn't come home last night?'

His body jilted with a humourless laugh.

'I wasn't the only one having a late night,' he said, mostly to himself.

Catherine moved a plastic chair near him and sat down on it, facing him.

'Ah good, I was hoping we didn't have to play funny buggers. So after you killed Frawley what was your next move?'

He looked at her, his eyes glazed.

'You don't know much.'

'I know you were with Frawley last night.'

He shifted his weight slowly.

'You don't know much else though. Leave me be. You're not a member of this club.'

He lazily gestured towards the door.

'You loved Cassandra. Don't you want to know what happened?'

He stared at her for a long time. 'How do you know I don't?'

The hairs on Catherine's neck saluted. 'So it's you.'

He grinned lazily. 'No. I'm not the one.'

'You had Frawley scared.'

Shiloh grinned and looked at the floor, his mouth working as he mulled over an idea. 'That was earlier. I wasn't the only one around Frawley. I'm sorry about the fat man getting hurt.' Suddenly he frowned, propping himself up on an elbow and looking at her. 'I'm also not the type to cut a man's eyes out. Sorry if I came across that way.'

It was by far the most genuine thing she had ever heard Shiloh say. She almost felt like apologising.

She took it as a sign to continue an aggressive line. She leaned forward in her chair.

'Are you sure? Athletic guy, fit and tough, about six foot, penchant for wearing black in the night? Can't be many of those around.'

Shiloh grunted. 'There's a bloody production line.'

'Why were you so afraid of what Frawley was going to expose?'

Shiloh sat up and leaned lazily against the couch.

'He was going to tell the world that Thoth was cruel to women and men, particularly women. That a small arsenal of writers wrote all our teachings. Supervised by Asher and me.' He cracked a knuckle, thoughtfully. 'It was going to sink us.'

'How was he going to do it? He's not a journalist.'

'He said he could find one.'

'I wouldn't have been worried by it. Your business would survive.'

Shiloh looked uncomfortable. 'It's an area where my brother and I have very differing views, you wouldn't understand.' He rubbed his face. 'No one understands.'

'A lot of it's true though, isn't it?'

'The bit about Thoth not being a guru is right.'

She took a step towards him. 'Is he dead?'

Shiloh looked at her, impassive, then turned away again.

'I doubt it.'

'Do you guide all the teachings?'

There was another long pause.

'We go in waves. One year we will be very aggressive and push a new set of meditations and retreats, the next we won't. This is a non-push year. We haven't done a great deal. Father showed us this way. It keeps you mysterious. Nothing worse than a pushy guru. We coordinate through our company all the individual countries we work in.'

'Can I ask a question that may seem stupid?'

'Another one? Why not?'

'Your charm is consistent, sir. Couldn't you just become the new guru? Say your father's spirit is gone to the eternal Om of our ancestors, he placed his hands upon his son and I am now the divine Hamburger, officially?'

'Two words – Julian Lennon.'

'Oh, right.' He wasn't a stupid man, he just had terrible manners.

'Why did Cassandra want to expose you?'

'Because I wouldn't do something. But she's dead now.'

'You were lovers.'

He shot her a contemptuous look. 'Piss off.'

'Is this yours?' She threw the ring.

Shiloh looked at it for a long time. Catherine thought he would cry. Then he spoke, very quietly: 'She wanted me to marry her. I wouldn't because of Asher.'

Catherine said nothing. There didn't seem much to say.

'As for the stuff about Dad,' Shiloh said. 'We don't make much of a secret of it, but it's the kind of thing that if it got in the papers would ruin us, especially if they connected it to the unfortunate stuff twenty years ago. Asher disagrees, but he has no head for business. She'd done a deal for a book, with spreads in the weekend papers no doubt. No going back. Can you imagine, if the book came out it would be devoured by every sceptic, every annoyed husband of a wife determined to start breathing prahna. The profits would diminish.'

Catherine was always turned off by people talking about profits, so she changed the subject.

'I believe Cassandra loved to get a reaction out of people.'

'Just people who couldn't handle her. Like my brother.'

Shiloh took out a small pouch and began rolling another joint.

Catherine leaned in, trying to make him look away from his drugs. 'They were lovers; no one can handle their own lover. It seems you couldn't either.'

Shiloh laughed at this. Outside, the light was fading fast. He went on.

'She could handle him. They were a strange pair, him in New Age, her in real estate. I can't tell you how often she would quietly wind him up and then get this amazing smile on her face when he lost his temper. It was an awesome sight. No one has ever been able to match my brother like that.'

Catherine thought of the hundreds of lost foot races Shiloh had run against Asher, and she began to see why he would be so fond of Cassandra, how he could be her lover as well as her pseudo brother-in-law.

Catherine leaned back in her chair. 'I spoke to someone earlier today who thinks your father might have killed her.'

Shiloh's eyebrows raised in unison.

'Thoth is here?'

'I haven't seen him, have you?'

Shiloh began to stand up; it was obviously an effort.

'No, but it would make sense. Things have been difficult recently.'
Catherine was on her feet, too. 'What's been so hard, Shiloh?'
Shiloh lit his smoke. 'Lots of jobs recently.'
'What jobs?'
'Follow up on debt, move some stocks around.'
As he spoke he put his shoes on. Fingers fumbling slightly. He looked up at Catherine and spoke out the side of his mouth. 'Follow a fat man. Cut a doll. That kind of thing.' He grinned like a wolf.
'Cut a doll to frame a woman?' Indignation gave her voice an edge.
'Yes. You never thought the witch killed her, I know. Wasn't me either. I just know that I'd been told to put the doll in place.'
'By who?'
'By a ghost who wanted insurance.' He laughed. 'Don't worry, I've had my sulk. It's time to sort it all out.'
Catherine moved closer to him, close enough to enjoy the smell. 'And you didn't tell the police?'
'Without the witch in the frame it would fall to my brother or me. Unacceptable. Father made sure we were close. Plus, I couldn't believe it would be him.'
'What does that mean?' she asked his back as he walked towards the door. She followed him urgently.
He turned his head towards her. Took a long drag and exhaled the smoke slowly. He raised a hand towards his face and began, 'It means…' then the crack snapped through the air, a window smashed and his body fell backwards, tumbling into itself and landing at an impossible angle.
The room remained absolutely quiet, in the absence of the incredible noise of the shot. Catherine became aware of the fresh air coming through the shattered window. Her eyes darted to the body; Shiloh's dead gaze was staring up from around his shoulder, the head twisted almost completely around, chest to the floor. Catherine looked to the window. A dark movement flashed in twilight. She ran through the door, hurling herself through the dark change rooms to the outside. She turned left towards the place where the shot came from. Running towards a gun that had just killed a man in front of her. Ignoring her rational mind asking, why on earth would she do this?
Within a minute she was underneath the broken window. Again the scene seemed painfully normal, with cars passing just a hundred metres away on Victoria Street. There was even the sound of people playing

tennis on the nearby courts. She steadied herself and looked back to the broken window, the only evidence she had not imagined the whole terror of Shiloh being killed in front of her. Her eyes darted around, looking for a clue, a hint. There was nothing, just the sound of a breeze rattling broken window glass.

15

So much of the universe is silence; I don't know why that scares us.
~ Asher Marr

Aside from traffic, the only movement outside was a mother pushing a pram through the small park that connected the oval to Victoria Street. Catherine walked slowly, not wanting to run into a bullet. Aware that she hadn't taken many breaths. The wind whistled through the leaves above her. The smell of grass was thick in her nostrils. Her mouth was bitter with adrenaline. She brought her phone out. Called 000. She spoke precisely, knowing the call was recorded. Saying a man had been shot in the pavilion of the Alex G. Gillon Oval. That the man's name was Shiloh Marr and that she had witnessed it. She hung up the phone. Later there would be questions, now there was only fear, for her and Asher.

She rang him, two rings, four rings.

'Hello?' Catherine almost doubled over. She could hear traffic.

'Asher, is your window open?'

'Yes, how did you…?'

'Close it, don't open the door to anyone but me. I'm coming now.'

She killed the line and found a knot in her gut unfurling. Sure he may find that emasculating, but if he's as evolved as he seems, he'll deal with it.

As she approached the road, a car drove past slowly, the driver and passenger not looking at her. Not looking suspicious. She set off running, still haunted by the anticipated crack of a gun.

She had gone two hundred metres along the road, trying to make as little sound as possible. She kept to the darkness and crossed roads when there were no car headlights illuminating the road.

She ran, not an action that came easily to her, and each time her foot hit the ground she imagined Asher's face as he saw his killer. Would it look like his father? She thought of the fear she had seen on him when they had parted. After a minute adrenaline lost out to the stitch in her side but she pushed on, walking fast. It was only a half kilometre away. Visions of him dead, or dying, were playing continually in her head. Interspersed with images of him laughing and walking with her in an autumn in France. For all her scorn of his panic she was filled with a viscous dread that she wasn't able to shake. At that moment, she had wanted more than anything for Asher to be saved and for that beautiful face to be preserved, for her and for the planet forever. She thought again of her own father, the quiet genius of a man. Compared to most men he was a giant; compared to Thoth he was a saint. She really should give him a call sometime.

She approached the shop from the west side of the tracks, moving through underbrush, away from the bike path, and away from prying eyes. When she saw the shop there were no dark figures, no guns, no police. She stood and watched carefully before she moved forward. The evening seemed practically comatose compared to the manic pace of her brain.

The only people who looked at her as she walked briskly to the door were a pair of drunken tradies, stumbling towards the Union Hotel. Catherine murmured thanks to the powers that be and rummaged in her small bag.

She let herself in with the key Asher had given her. 'Yep, he's a keeper,' she muttered as she frantically turned the key in the lock. Some cooler part of her brain remembered the first time she had stood at this door, not so long ago. It hit her that even if he were unharmed, she would have to tell Asher that his brother was dead. She paused for a second, halfway through the shop. She had never lost a sibling, but could imagine. A shiver rose through her and she was glad she had the moment alone.

The shop and adjoining stock room were silent. Catherine walked on the balls of her feet, padding as quietly as she could. She balled her hands and climbed the stairs into the light above.

Asher was staring out the window, closed as requested, as she rose up the stairs. Catherine felt a promise quietly grow in her chest as she stopped to look at him. He held a glass in his hand, and there was a stillness about him. She was impressed by the power that exuded from his stance. She wondered how she could have worried for him. He turned, walked over and embraced her. Catherine allowed herself to be swept up by him. He smelled like all the best things in the world.

'Asher.'

He kissed her, long and lovingly. She didn't want it to finish. It was another good kiss. She liked kissing him; she liked the way his lips and mouth moved. She also liked that while he kissed her she didn't have to tell him. But then he said it.

'You found him.' It didn't look like fear in his eyes.

'Yes.'

'Is he?'

'He's dead.'

He made a noise like a hurt child. His eyes closed. Catherine touched his face, saying nothing. There was nothing she could say and she knew it. All she could do was be with him, and tell the truth.

She told him, clinically and surgically what had happened. Taking her time so as not to miss details. He stared at her as she spoke, tears rolling slowly down his face. When she talked about the shot, he bit his fist.

Catherine wanted to push for them to leave, now. She watched him instead. Asher looked around the room, closed his eyes and drew in a deep breath. He let it out and looked at her, back in control. His voice was steady, but quiet. 'Was he happy?'

'He wasn't sad.'

Asher sat down at a nearby table seat. Then he looked up at Catherine quickly. 'We're in danger.'

'Yes.' She knew it wouldn't take him long. He stood.

'We should leave. We should leave now.'

Catherine was unable to think of a reason why not. With Shiloh dead, surely the police couldn't hold Melissa any longer. There was no harm in leaving while the police rounded up the killer. It would be the responsible thing to do.

'Where to?'

'Toulouse, right?'

Catherine wrinkled her nose, despite herself. 'It's getting too cold there now.'

'How about Spain, then?'

'Sounds better.'

Asher ran to his room to pick up his passport and some clothes. Catherine's own, which she always kept with her for such occasions, was in her bag. She called Boris and left a message that Shiloh was dead and she was leaving town with Asher to avoid a similar fate. She would have called Mel but it would be hours before she'd be out. There would be some emails to send from Spain, and some bridges to rebuild in the hat-making world. That didn't matter as much as keeping Asher safe.

Gentle hands crossed over her shoulders and ran down her sides, taking their time about it. She leaned back into his embrace. She listened to him breathe. She turned and he seemed to be glowing; she placed a hand on his chest and ran it across his left side, feeling a desire rise that they couldn't afford. She was about to suggest calling a cab when he kissed her. Alive, flickering and temporary.

Just as they kissed, Catherine heard a faint tinkle of glass. Asher obviously hadn't heard it and was making intense contact with the back of her dress. Then he noticed she had stiffened in alarm. She mouthed the word, 'downstairs'.

He visibly paled and moved towards the trap door that led to the shop. A further bump came from downstairs and he looked back at her. Catherine went towards the kitchen, searching for a decent sized knife. Asher didn't seem to be the type to have a cricket bat.

She thought about Thoth, and that she usually enjoyed meeting a beau's father. Strange times.

Asher approached the closed trapdoor like a cat, his fingers splayed. He looked like a ballet dancer playing a duelling cowboy. Sounds of footsteps and breathing came from the stock room, and it occurred to Catherine that whoever killed Cassandra, Frawley and Shiloh couldn't have been this clumsy. She relaxed a little and moved to flank Asher, eyes still looking for an impromptu weapon.

The trap door opened and there emerged Alice. She was breathing heavily, with a trickle of blood running down her forearm, likely from breaking the glass. The nose was, as usual, unmistakable and she was wearing the same clothes as earlier in the day. The most changed part of her was her eyes. The drugs had truly worn off and Alice was enraged, her shoulders rising and falling impossibly for such a small woman. Catherine's hindquarters throbbed slightly with the sight of their tormentor, but Alice was not the terrifying force that Thoth would have been.

Asher had almost pounced when the door opened, but now he looked aghast.

'You?' His eyes squinted in disgust.

Alice spat, pointing her finger at Asher's chest. Blood dripped slowly from her fingers. 'You have hidden the signs enough, you have obscured the light and twisted the shadow, and you will burn.'

'What in God's name are you talking about, woman? I remember you, you were father's...'

Catherine wondered why Asher was suddenly talking like he was in the sixteenth century. Alice's pantomime act was obviously contagious.

'You thought to show the Father had returned, but like Cain you could not hide all your sins.'

Asher pointed at her: 'Did you kill Cassandra? Did you kill Shiloh?' He was walking backwards in a circle with Alice moving in front of him. Catherine, for once, was unsure what to do. The idea that Alice was the killer seemed absurd. She watched as this strange dance continued. Alice's hand gripped Asher's shirt as she screamed.

'I've shed no blood, I've freed no souls, though mine is always tormented by the wrath of the father. I saw much of the father in you, too. But no, your blood runs as cold as that of Haborym.'

Another drop of Alice's blood fell to the floor and Catherine came forward. The woman was clearly in pain. She took Alice's hand from Asher's chest and looked deep into her green eyes.

'Alice, we're all in danger, please breathe.'

Alice looked past her.

'You have been blinded by lust. The boy is cold. His seed is black. I see it now, he must have taken her to the alley, he must have pushed her against the wall.'

Asher moved past Catherine towards the witch.

'Enough.' The cry came from his lips as the back of his right wrist flashed across Alice's face. She fell to the floor.

'Asher.' Catherine's voice was husky with quiet rage. He turned away. Catherine helped Alice to her feet as Asher paced away, massaging his fist.

'She breaks into my house after my brother dies. I should give her more. Better father had killed her thirty years ago.'

Alice pushed away from Catherine and approached Asher with her finger outstretched. 'You have curved the blood of others to your will; you have betrayed the father's message. You will burn. As they all burn. You killed the brother and gave the death to your father's fate. I have seen it in the water and the flame. I wrote in red that the father had come but it was only the son riding a tide of blood.'

Asher stood impervious, looking like he would hit her again. Catherine was watching this, listening in case Alice was the decoy for Thoth entering and killing them. She was mesmerised by Alice's words, but also aware of the revulsion she felt when Asher had struck Alice.

She watched him and the same stance which minutes ago had seemed so proud, now looked arrogant. His eyes did seem cold. She felt that all too familiar sinking feeling the moment you realise that the man you've been kissing is a prick. He isn't really deep and complicated; he's just a prick. She suddenly wanted to get Alice, and herself, as far away from this man as possible.

'Come on Alice, let me get you home.'

The witch ignored her. Asher looked briefly at Catherine, saw the disdain on her face and did not seem perturbed by it. Alice continued speaking flowery accusations. Catherine didn't feel too compelled to cut short her tongue lashing.

'The father was always disappointed with you. He knew you were too eager for glory, too happy with your looks and your wiles. You will be found out, you will be found and you will burn. The father hated you. The father hated you.'

With these last words Alice was practically screaming. Catherine saw for a tiny second the warning look; she had seen it before in other men. She should have known Asher would be a slow burn bomb. It was the look that you only ever saw when it was too late.

Asher's mask fell away revealing only rage; Catherine tried to pull Alice away but was too late. Asher was as quick as anyone Catherine had ever seen.

Also, he had a knife. From somewhere in his clothes it came, pearl handled and as long as a hand. Catherine had barely registered it before it was plunged in Alice's belly and then up towards her heart. She fell back against Catherine. Asher's face came close to the witch's face and he spat, 'Tonight I feel like watching.'

As he spoke, Alice's hands moved in front of his face, the movement somehow familiar. Possibly a spell, possibly a defence.

Alice vomited up blood on her clothes and Catherine held her, tasting adrenaline again. She tried to run, but Alice had her in a death grip. She looked up from the blood to see Asher's left fist flying.

She thought of Daffy Duck and then there was nothing.

The bar was always busy on a Friday, but tonight it was especially full. The band was good and the college crowd were in full swing. All rugby jumpers and bravado. Boris didn't mind them. They were young, they were happy and they knew best. He'd hated their kind when he was studying but he found that as he got older he hated fewer and fewer people. Especially after the rather excellent parmigiana he had enjoyed for his staff meal, just thirty minutes before. The clock was moving along nicely, there were – for once – enough pints in the racks and unless he was completely out of his mind, that girl in the red cardigan kept insisting on being served by him.

He was surprised when he checked his phone that he'd missed a call from Catherine. He was further surprised to find a message from her on the Glasgow Palace's message machine.

'Hi Boris, sorry to call at work. Shiloh's dead. Shot. I was with him. I think it's probably Thoth. I'm going to Spain with Asher as soon as a cab arrives and I'll call you from there. I'm whisking him to safety by the way, not the other way round. They've got to let Melissa go now. Just be ready if the police come wanting to chat to you. Bye!' Boris didn't bother waiting for the beep.

As for the news of Shiloh dying, Boris shrugged his shoulders. Pretty soon Melissa would be released from prison, he and Catherine would be released from duty and the police could catch the Thoth guy whenever they got around to it.

And yes indeed, here was red cardigan girl again. Either she was buying all the rounds for her table or Boris Shakhovskoy was in with a chance. She was gorgeous too, long chestnut hair, lovely skin and a slightly gummy grin that only seemed to get bigger with each round.

'Same again?' Boris tilted the pint glass. He loved a girl who drank pints; they made his heart sing.

'Please.'

Boris set to work, waiting until Leon was finished with the front beer taps rather than taking the glass round to the back bar while she waited. No use in running away from a pretty girl.

'You were at the funeral, weren't you?'

'I'm sorry?' Boris looked up from the foaming drink he was pouring.

'Cassandra Pierce's funeral. I saw you there.'

'Yeah, that's right. Real shame that.'

'I didn't know her very well, how about you?'

'More of a friend of a friend. It's a sav blanc as well, right?' Boris smiled, he hoped mysteriously.

'Right.'

Boris poured the wine, making the portion as generous as he could with Leon lurking. He was unsure where to go from funerals and so just tried to look competent, his fallback position when it came to women.

Red Cardigan went on though, sparing him the trouble of thinking of something else.

'I was looking for you at the wake afterwards.'

'Were you? That's nice.' He smiled in the direction of a bar mat as if he'd been tickled.

'You have a nice face.'

Oh, it was a great night indeed. 'Comes from my mother. Thanks. I didn't get to the wake, had to work. I hear it went pretty wild?'

Red cardigan smiled. 'Yeah, nothing like a death to bring out the no tomorrow mentality.'

'I hear the boyfriend was a write-off.'

'Asher? Oh no. He left about 7.30.'

'Oh, really?'

'Yeah, my friend was looking for him,' she gestured to her table. 'She thinks he's…well, very attractive.'

Boris shrugged. 'But he wasn't there?' He was starting to feel anxious.

'No, he was nowhere to be seen. Hey, what time do you finish?'

Suddenly Boris' face drained of blood. He was standing very straight and very still. If the god of fate had been standing there at that time, Boris would have kicked him full blown in the testicles. He, Boris Seamus Shakhovskoy, son of Petrov and Mariah Shakhovskoy, had been a barman for the better part of a decade. In that time he had waited, so very patiently waited, for a beautiful member of the opposite sex to ask him that glimmering, wonderful question: What time do you finish? Or, even better, more alluring and suggestive: 'What time do you get off?' Either was fine. Now, tonight, a girl had asked him that but at the same time given him information that meant Catherine was in danger. That she was, in fact, currently in the arms of a man who had lied to her and who possibly had killed three or more people. He took a deep breath.

'What's your name?'

'Liese.'

'Liese, I finish in half an hour, and any other night of my life I would love to meet you and drink with you. But I'm afraid tonight I have to go to another job.'

'Oh, that's OK,' she said brightly, 'Does he finish then, too?' She pointed at Jimmy, the chef. 'He's beautiful.'

Boris smiled grimly, grabbing his phone and jacket and looking for Leon before he ran out the door. I will kill fate, he thought. It will be burned by flowers.

16

Men are either nice or interesting.
~ Britt Houden

At first there were just colours and a dull ache. Flashes of light like deep-sea fish, glowing just out of sight. She was desperately aware she had to do something, but couldn't yet because she had to find the right ribbon. Was it ribbon? Was it wire?

Then sounds came, a steady rhythm, with random bumps and sighs. After a time she realised the steady sound was her own breath. She blinked, then she remembered her name and the day, and was annoyed. It wasn't shaping up to be the world's greatest Friday. As she looked around the room she thought of Frawley.

A few minutes later she was fully awake. Bound but thankfully not gagged, plus she was still clothed, a relief. She was still in Asher's living room, staring at the skylight. No sign of stars tonight. Catherine shut her eyes a couple more times and tried to assess the damage to her head. Her vision in her right eye seemed a little blurry, and yes, her head hurt. But she still didn't feel half as bad as any time she mistakenly drank Kahlua.

Asher was a bastard. He'd played her all along and she had fallen for it. It would have been better had he revealed himself earlier, but now, when she had decided he was innocent, it just showed how truly stupid she had been. She had ignored Neal, Boris and her own gut, and for what? A pash with a man who hurt women. Her stomach turned as she recalled just how much of her brain she'd allowed to be taken up with fantasies of him. For a second she thought of her parents and how they would look in church at her funeral. Panic rose and she instinctively pushed it back. Panic was good for nothing; regrets could be dealt with later, if she lived. She could make her dad, Boris, and herself proud if she died well now.

Her hands were bound across her back, not particularly painfully; her feet were done too. As she looked towards them she saw Alice's body across the room. She shook her head. As far as annoying boyfriends went, Asher was well on his way to hitting her top ten.

A noise near her head made her look up; Asher was emerging from the trap door. His eyes looked like they were lit from within. How had she missed how much he enjoyed being a bastard? He looked so happy. He'd even changed his shirt into a deep red. If he started speaking in rhyme and invoking the power of the moon it couldn't make the situation worse.

'Glad you're awake. I was just making sure we're not disturbed.' He looked at Alice and shook his head. 'Silly bloody witch poked a hole in the window and unlocked the door. That won't happen now.'

He flexed his back, as if taking a tension away, or limbering up. 'We're safe as houses.'

'Asher, you sound like such a creep, who are you trying to impress?'

If he kept this crap up he'd be in the top five by midnight. Catherine thought of Boris having to knock off at the bar. Hurting him would be the worst part.

Asher pulled a small wooden stool from a corner and sat close to her left elbow, picking at a piece of loose leather on his boot. 'I really was going to take you to Spain. I started out thinking I'd kill you too, since you were so nosy, but I began to enjoy myself. Strange.'

'So you killed Cassandra, framed Melissa, and made Shiloh back up your alibi just to keep your daddy's business safe?'

'Daddy.' Asher was grinning to himself and playing with the knife, running the flat across his hands. 'Maybe Alice is right and I am a great disappointment to Thoth. When you spend your whole life being so deep it's hard to know what anyone really thinks, you know? I wish you could have come to some of the seminars I run. I can play all the parts. I learned that from Thoth himself.'

He stood up, rolling his neck slowly as if some drugs were coming on. 'I can be anything you want me to be.'

Catherine wanted to hear about Thoth; and to keep him talking. 'Oh, is your father in on all this? Is he waiting in the cupboard to clap you on the back and make you vice-president of The Way? Was Shiloh less murdered than moved on?'

Thud. Catherine hadn't seen it coming, the knife was stuck fast into the wooden floorboards just centimetres from her face. The knife looked stronger than it ever had on Melissa's kitchen wall. That was the total sum of her thoughts: the knife looked strong and her buttocks were still itchy. She could have rolled, or tried to roll, if she had had any idea that he was about to throw it. Asher moved slowly towards her and pulled the knife from the floor as he spoke.

'Catherine, I killed Thoth years ago. I couldn't stand that sanctimonious bastard.'

'Right.' The back of Catherine's head hit the floor as she exhaled. Oh, well. Everyone blows it eventually. 'So it wasn't business?'

'Nope.' He was back to pacing, stroking his knife in a way that Catherine was glad he had never stroked her. 'It wasn't business. Just personal, and pleasure.

'Cassandra was just pushing and pushing, always gloating that she could make me lose my temper. One day, she would say, one day I'll win. We fought about other women, the book she would write about us. Then she tried to hurt me, with my poor stupid brother.' He looked at her. 'You worked that bit out?'

Catherine nodded. Couldn't see the point in playing dumb.

'I had to put a stop to it. All I had to do was leave enough clues so that no one realised I was behind all of it. Cassandra thought I was bluffing, Frawley thought it was Shiloh, the police thought it was Melissa and you, well you just got scared of my evil, mysterious Father. I just kept telling Shiloh to push Frawley to scare you away. Then when it turned out you weren't just a stupid girl, I had to kill Frawley or he might have talked and you could have wound it back to me. When Shiloh found out about Frawley I could see his loyalty was slipping. Plus, I think he was working out that dad was never coming back. Remember how angry he was when you first met him?'

Catherine closed her eyes. 'You had just told him.'

'Not about Thoth, just that I had killed Cassandra and that he had planted a key piece of evidence, and even stolen the murder weapon. I had wondered about framing the witch, so I had Shiloh put the doll in her house and take the knife. He thought I was just playing the witch, but I was laying a trail of crumbs for the cops.'

'Why did he go along with it?'

'Because he knew I could hurt him.' He smiled. 'Shiloh was easy enough about making Frawley squirm, and it was him at the office who knocked you over, but it was me in Frawley's car. It was me who twisted the knife on that pathetic soul. Shiloh even got angry about the eyes thing, but I knew that I had to keep the witch-hunt going. He was so crazy this morning I was worried he was going to the police.' He stopped walking. 'But then he called me on the brother phone.'

'You sent me there.'

'I sent you to watch.'

'Why?'

'I wanted you to solve the mystery; make you think it was my wicked father. Tell your fat friend and the police. I wanted to make you believe the myth of Thoth. I wanted to see if I could make the police think that Catherine had done their job for them. While I had you in Barcelona.' He ran a hand along her cheek. 'There's still time if you want.'

'Hands off.'

He laughed and sat on his stool again. 'Do you know what I love, Catherine?'

'Probably Neil Diamond.'

'I love pushing people in to the places I want them. It's a game I've been playing all my life. People will do anything if they think it will get them the truth.'

Catherine had to concede the point, though not verbally.

'You probably always knew that the booze would get you one day.'

This was too much. 'If you're going to make me a gin and tonic, I'll listen to this for another five minutes, but if not, kindly pull your finger out and stab me.' Catherine's guts were churning and she was aware at some point her nerve might fail.

Asher chuckled, completely at ease. 'All I had to do was drink some salt water so I'd vomit at your feet and tell you how hungover I was. You didn't even check with anyone from the wake.'

It hadn't been Catherine's best day. She'd have shrugged if she weren't tied up.

'So where are her fingers?'

'What?'

'Sorry to interrupt the gloating, but you're a wanker. What happened to Cassandra's fingers?'

'Same as Frawley's eyes. There's a house just a block from here that keeps a pig, those things eat anything. Nothing too brilliant or sinister.' He looked at his watch.

'Now,' he leant close to Catherine, 'if you give me a kiss I'll do it quick for you.'

Catherine thought for a moment of Boris. Of all the things she would miss. He brought a smile to her lips and for a second she was sure she could hear his voice.

'I don't kiss cowards.'

He laughed as if that were the grandest thing he had ever heard.

'You're a feisty one. I think you and Cassandra would have got along.'

'She told Shiloh he was the better lover. Sorry to disappoint.'

It was beneath her, but it was all she had.

Asher stopped, looked at his knife and smiled. 'Lust, truth, meaning. They all blind you from what life is about.'

'What's that?'

'Death for the weak, power for the killers.' The blade flashed as the light reflected off it.

It was then she heard the sound of breaking glass and the scream of an orgasming polar bear. Asher looked up as Boris fell through the skylight.

Catherine had just enough feeling left in her arms and legs to roll away a second before the glass fell. It was mostly shattered, though a few long shards rained onto the floorboards and jutted out, one rather cruelly into Alice's chest, though she didn't seem to notice. Boris, ever the stuntman, had made sure his fall was broken by Asher. The killer was knocked sideways and fell against the stool, which broke under the impact of the two bodies. Catherine turned to watch them struggle together, sliding on her buttocks away from the scuffle. Asher was clearly stunned, and looked more than a little annoyed to have his game interrupted, but he was by far the more agile and he had managed to keep a grip on his knife. He pushed the big man off him, unfazed, before Boris landed a punch squarely on his jaw. Asher staggered, but Boris was hurt. He was limping badly.

Boris made the mistake of moving towards Catherine. His eyes were wild, and blood dripped down his face on the left side. Asher rose up behind him like a closing panther.

'Turn around man, he'll stab you!'

Catherine was wrong again. It was one of those nights. Asher, still staggering, had simply put his foot into the small of Boris' back and kicked him towards Catherine. Boris skidded across the floor and rolled, landing close to Catherine.

He shook his head and looked up to see Asher, knife out, advancing.

Boris wiped sweat from his eyes.

'I told you this guy was a prick.'

Catherine writhed in her bonds. 'For once I'm not in a position to argue.'

Asher looked incredulous. 'I'm going to enjoy killing both of you.'

Boris piped up behind his raised fists.

'In case I don't make it through this, did you kill everyone?'

Asher's hands moved fast again. Catherine didn't even see the knife. Neither did Boris, though he stood blinking as his shirt flapped open. The knife was stuck into the wall, four metres behind him. There was no cut on his body. The knife had only ripped his shirt.

Asher brought another knife from behind his back and licked the end of it.

Boris' face paled, but he raised his fists again.

'So, did you kill everyone?'

Asher rolled his eyes. 'Yes Boris. I killed everyone. I inherit everything, now I kill you. Then I move somewhere and drink cocktails all day. Got it?'

He raised the knife to throw it. Boris began moving in front of Catherine.

As he did, a strange look appeared on Asher's face. As if he suddenly smelled gas or remembered he had a cake in the oven. He shook it off and poised his hand again, moving the knife back to throw with Boris just metres away. As his wrist reached its zenith, Asher's face contorted. His left hand suddenly dropped to his buttock and grabbed at his trousers. Catherine remembered the hand movement Alice had made before she died, and realised when she had seen it before. Asher made a panicked sound, turned briefly to Boris and half-heartedly threw the knife. Boris ducked and the knife sailed into the leather couch.

'Boris, get him now,' Catherine said.

Boris rushed the thinner man, who was ripping at his dark pants and screaming in agony. As the glass crushed under his foot, Boris found the leg of the dark wooden stool, which he raised in an arc and crashed down onto Asher's head.

Asher Marr fell face down onto the glass, having managed to rip his trouser down to his thighs. Much of his torso was obscured to Catherine by Boris' panting body; in fact all she could see were a pair of tanned, very taut, very impressive buttocks, with a flower emerging on the left side.

There was a thump from the floor underneath them and the wail of police sirens was suddenly audible.

EPILOGUE

'It was an amazing thing.' Catherine was as close to slurring as she ever got.

'Which bit?' Boris was already there.

'All of it really, but I think I had the best view of the crucial moment.' Catherine's hands were flapping as she tried to clarify her thoughts.

'Hold on, hold on,' Melissa Zamansky raised both her hands, one of which held a cigarette and the other her phone. 'It's the third time you've told the story and I still don't know what happened really. I wasn't there. The magazines will want to know.'

Catherine rubbed her still sore wrists and looked around the Glasgow Palace's beer garden. It was a glorious day to be free and to be alive. With sunshine flooding the space and reflecting small prisms of colour from the glasses that were slowly accumulating in the centre of their table. Catherine gave Boris a look and began holding court.

'Boris, in his wisdom, had seen me tied up and had made a phone call to the boys in blue to head on down to rescue us, and then realised I wasn't going to last, so he sets his phone to record the confession and jumps. Then I got to see what a thirty thousand dollar skylight looks like as it's broken by a falling barman.'

'It was all I could think of. Don't make a big deal of it.'

Melissa took her eyes off her Twitter feed momentarily. 'So Alice's spell saved your bacon? Who'd have thought?'

Boris put down his pint. 'Oh yes, Alice. I jump to my doom and the dead witch...' He stopped. 'Oh wait, that's pretty callous. She can have the credit.' Shamefaced, he blessed himself.

Catherine chided him, 'Oh, Boris, you got a new scar, you saved me and you got the crucial piece of evidence. You can share the credit on this one.'

Boris rubbed his beard. 'Oh, right. Thanks.'

Melissa raised her mineral water. 'Thanks, you two. I'll never find out the long-term wonders of the big house,' she shuddered and then smiled as her phone buzzed with more twittering. She was already planning a book about her ordeal.

Boris looked about happily. 'So Catherine, what was that whole "burned by flowers" thing anyway? I even found myself saying it. Is that what happened to Asher? Did that happen to you first?'

Catherine gentle rattled the ice cubes in her glass. 'My dear Boris, I'll make you a deal. You go buy me another drink.'

'And?'

'I'll probably never tell you anyway.'

Three days later, Catherine was one of six people at Alice's funeral. It was short and sad, though fittingly done outdoors, giving a nod to her Wiccan beliefs. Tom, the rotund man from Stewart Lodge, cried through most of it. Catherine stood next to Kenneth Williams as the celebrant talked about Alice's life. The shared silence was among the more pleasant things Catherine had ever felt.

Afterwards, Catherine almost asked if he wanted a drink, but simply said goodbye.

Williams looked at her. 'Four dead. It's a bloody waste.'

'Could have been worse.'

'A lot worse. You know what?'

'What?'

'You could have been a real copper, Catherine.'

'You'd have made a terrible milliner.'

She liked that he was still chuckling as he drove away.

ACKNOWLEDGMENTS

A huge thanks to Lindy Cameron of Clan Destine Press, who has rescued Catherine and this book from being out of print. Narrelle Harris gave the work a further edit to bring it in line with the CDP ways.

The below acknowledgements I wrote five years ago when *Jinx* was first published. I should say that I'm still grateful to all these people.

Thanks to Threekookaburras founder Annie Hall, firstly for publishing *Jinx*, secondly for editing. Her efforts have improved the manuscript beyond measure. Sydney Smith also provided excellent advice which steered the book to publication. No one has worked on this book harder than Mardi O'Connor, who poured hours of time into early drafts and giving editing 101 lessons to a first time author. Joe Loh was the first to read the book in its earliest inception and gave great encouragement and criticism. Since then the work has been improved by the wisdom of T. B. McKenzie, Laila Fanebust, Andrew Croome, Lachlan Plain and Dusty Treweek. Marissa Zawadsky showed me magic, lent me books and didn't mind me basing a character on her and then twisting it far out of recognition. Carrie O'Shea gave great counsel on the criminal justice system, and agreed to be on call to answer 'bloody stupid questions' while juggling a Herculean caseload within that very system. June Edwards taught me millinery basics and proved to me once and for all that class struggle can indeed look fabulous. Agent K was kind enough to provide detailed insight into crime scene investigation. My wonderful friend and doctor, PCD schooled me on the possibilities and limitations of the recently deceased, without such advice the book would have remained ludicrous. My writing group gave regular, frank and supportive feedback throughout the drafting and have all made great improvements to the work. These marvellous human beings include Clare Bowditch, Peggy Frew, Rachel Powers, Louisa Syme, Michael Dwyer, Jack Cassidy, Mardi O'Connor, Kate Ryan and Sally Rippin. My band have been very patient with me through this process. Adam, Phil and Ryan are the loveliest rogues you could ever be stuck in a small room with. Andrea and Hugh McGinlay brought me up in a house full of books, which is a wonderful gift. Any part of this book that made you laugh shows the influence of my brother Danny. My children, Eliza and Cormac, teach me what is important. Lastly, I would like to thank my wonderful wife Louise, who lights up the world, brightens the corners and makes me laugh every day.

HUGH McGINLAY

Hugh is a writer and musician. These poor career choices means that he has also worked as a bus driver, a kitchenhand, singing teacher and a seller of dental consumables. He loves lying in hammocks, rereading books and walking around airports holding a guitar case.

He lives in Melbourne with his wife Louise, their two children, a cat and six chickens.

www.ingramcontent.com/pod-product-compliance
Lightning Source LLC
Chambersburg PA
CBHW020650260626
47157CB00008B/2983